R. C. Farrington

Illustrated by Jason Farrington

Copyright © 2016 Rodney Farrington

All Rights Reserved

www.bermudaspinners.com

ISBN-13: **978-153978564-4**
ISBN-10: **1539785645**

Library of Congress Control Number: 2016914651
CreateSpace Independent Publishing Platform, North Charleston, SC

Jason Farrington has created outstanding graphic designs for this novel. www.7summitscreative.com

I would like to dedicate this book to my grandchildren, Lorynn, Sadie, Alexandra, and of course those other grandchildren who have yet to join us. This adventure is for them to read when they are able and to let their imaginations run wild. Who knows? Maybe someday they'll sit down with their own children and let them discover a world that their papa envisioned just for them to explore. After all, as I say, life is an adventure.

Characters depicted in this novel other than known historical persons are all fictitious. Comparisons to people living in the past or present are coincidental and not intentional.

Contents

Introduction.................................7
1 The Upheaval..............................8
2 The Spinners.............................13
3 The Invasion............................17
4 The City of Atlantis....................27
5 Captured................................33
6 Waterfall of Death......................43
7 The Escape..............................48
8 The Black Lake..........................54
9 The Labyrinth...........................61
10 A Lost Friend..........................66
11 Skull Mountain.........................73
12 Welcome to Hades.......................79
13 The Fortress of the Dredge.............83
14 The Lost Empire........................89
15 The Night of the Dredge................96
16 Point of No Return....................105
17 No Way Out............................112
18 Mystery Cove..........................122
19 The Dark Tunnel.......................133
20 The Crystal Cavern....................148
21 The Journey Back to Atlantis..........157
22 The Valley of Darkness................163
23 Time Is Running Out...................172
24 A Guide from Within...................177
25 Which Way Out?........................182
26 Cavern of Dreams......................193
27 The Trap..............................203
28 The Voyage............................214

29 The Forgotten Land..........................221
30 Trapped..227
31 The Last Stand.................................234
32 The Final Upheaval..........................240
33 The Crystal Spinner.........................248
34 Homeward Bound............................255

Introduction

For thousands of years, storytellers have told the tale of the lost city of Atlantis. There are thousands of stories and tales of this lost world and its inhabitants. Reports of the lost city's location range from the Mediterranean Sea to the Sargasso Sea. Some describe Atlanteans as super beings, and some describe them as giants.

Descriptions of the tragic end to this advanced civilization have thousands of variations that no one can agree on. With no real evidence and only handed-down stories and the imaginations of storytellers and writers, most consider the lost city of Atlantis simply another story passed on through the ages.

I will not waste your time with the story of the lost city of Atlantis. You can read a hundred other novels about Atlantis. No, this novel is not about the lost city or tales about the past; it's about the found city of Atlantis. Yes, Atlantis does exist. Sit back, relax, and enjoy your adventure in a place where no man or woman has gone for thousands of years.

Chapter 1
The Upheaval

The Upheaval

Bermuda, the island, has not always been in its long, jagged, curved shape. At the time before the Great Upheaval, it was more like most islands today. It was more of an oval shape. Thousands of years ago, the island of Bermuda was in fact the island city of Atlantis. On the night of the Great Upheaval, everything changed for this tiny island-state.

That night the storytellers spun the tale of the island exploding and destroying all the inhabitants of the island. That was not the case. What did happen was an earthshaking upheaval that caused two-thirds of the island to sink beneath the surface of the ocean. The upheaval struck like lightning; it gave no warning and no chance of escape. In minutes, the upheaval was over, and the city of Atlantis was gone with it. No, the city was not lost but transformed into a subterranean city beneath the ocean floor, where it exists today.

Today geologists tell us that the makeup of Bermuda is a mixture of an ancient volcano and coral that was formed over the years. All this is true. These distinct differences in the island's makeup have created two cultures miles beneath Bermuda. Beneath the island of Bermuda, there are two separate kingdoms. One kingdom is encased in coral and crystal. The other kingdom is encased in remnants of the ancient volcano that once dominated the island.

The inhabitants of the coral and crystal kingdom are the Atlanteans. Yes, their kingdom is called Atlantis. Although life today is nothing like it was in their golden age, they still stay loyal to their traditions and past.

When Atlantis was on the surface thousands of years ago, because of its location, it was truly a melting pot of cultures and races. This free population was equally made up of Greeks, Europeans, Asians, and Africans. But due to isolation over thousands of years, the population is now blended into one.

It's hard for us to believe, but after living beneath the sea for thousands of years, their skin color is a beautiful golden, light-brown tone. The artificial light from the huge crystal deposits has helped keep them healthy without the side effects of direct sunlight. Life in this city is much like life in any other city, but the true focus of Atlanteans is on maintaining the balance of the crystal pendulum.

The crystal pendulum hangs from the ceiling of the massive Great Crystal Hall. The pendulum aligns directly over a razor-sharp, triangular, pointed, black magnetic stone. As long as the points of the stone and pendulum are directly touching each other, all is well in the Sargasso Sea. The surface area of these two points is no more than one-thirty-second of an inch. Once these points disconnect, unusual happenings begin to occur in the Sargasso Sea.

The Atlanteans call these mini upheavals, whereas surface inhabitants call this phenomenon the effects of the Bermuda Triangle. Many people believe that the Bermuda Triangle is a parallel world where people, ships, and aircraft are lost.

In reality, the Bermuda Triangle is an area in the Sargasso Sea that is affected by the crystal pendulum. Thus the Bermuda Triangle is not a place but the result of a condition caused by the crystal pendulum being out of sync. The more the pendulum swings off its base point of center, the more the Bermuda Triangle wreaks havoc in the Sargasso Sea and thus causes aircraft, ships, and people to be lost at sea.

The ruler of Atlantis is the young Princess Ariadne. She is a slender young lady with long silky black hair that glistens in the crystal light. Her parents were killed long ago by the Dredge when she was just a few years old. On her eighteenth birthday, which is only a month away, she will be crowned Queen Ariadne of Atlantis. She is the last of her bloodline and the only person who knows the secrets of the crystal pendulum. The Dredge know this and have plotted for months to capture her and take her prisoner and destroy the pendulum, thus ending the power of the pendulum.

The Dredge are the inhabitants of the volcanic kingdom of Undercroft, which is defined in the Greek language as "a vault or chamber under the ground." Many years after the Upheaval, Atlantis found itself in the throes of a war.

A band of renegade Atlanteans tried to overthrow the king. These Atlanteans believed themselves to be superior to the rest of the population and wanted a Spartan existence.

After several years of war, the Dredge were defeated and exiled from the Atlantis. They were forced to live in the volcanic part of the underworld, which is now known as the Undercroft Kingdom.

The Dredge have never forgiven the Atlanteans for their exile. They are always seeking weaknesses or cracks in the Atlantis walls. The Dredge are very different than the Atlanteans. The Dredge skin is grayish and very chapped and dried out. Almost like bark on a tree. Their diet is mostly mushrooms, mold and bugs. Anything that is clean and bright they destroy.

The lord of Undercroft is Styx. In Undercroft, there is no line of succession. The most ruthless, cutthroat, alpha male in the dark kingdom will probably always be the ruler, as is the case now. Styx is the most brutal man in Undercroft and has managed to maintain his death grip on the Dredge kingdom for years.

He is very aware of Princess Ariadne's coming-of-age and will stop at nothing to prevent that. Styx has no intention of invading and ruling Atlantis. He is obsessed with destroying Atlantis and the pendulum. He has been waiting patiently for the right time, and he believes that the time will be soon.

Chapter 2
The Spinners

The Spinners

Back on the surface world in Bermuda, a small group of teenagers, completely unaware of the two worlds beneath them, is going about the daily summer routine of exploring Bermuda. This is not just any group of teenagers. They all have a special bond and call themselves the Spinners.

Michael Clark is an American from Boston. He visits Bermuda every summer and stays with his grandmother. Michael is thirteen years old and wishes he could live in Bermuda year round.

Keno Ming is dark skinned and is very large and powerful for his fourteen years of age. He lives at the St. David's lighthouse, where his father is the lighthouse keeper.

Samantha (Sam) Savage is a beautiful and brilliant young girl. She is thirteen years old and is considered the brains of the group. Her father is Inspector Ian Savage, a local police inspector for the St. George's branch of the Bermuda police force.

Roderick (Portagee) Madeiros is the littlest and the youngest, at twelve years old, but he is an inventive Portuguese boy and an electronic whiz kid.

Graham Aston is dark skinned and also thirteen years old. He's the rich kid of the group. His family is the dominant oil importer in Bermuda.

Every day is a new adventure for them.

On this day, they were going skink hunting in a rocky area of Tom Moore's jungle. They weren't really going to catch any. They just wanted to watch them in their habitat. Skinks are a species of rock lizards. They are much larger than a regular lizard and look a little slimy. This species of lizard is considered endangered in Bermuda.

As they entered Tom Moore's jungle, Portagee said, "I'll lead the way. I can get us there quickly."

Sam quickly spoke up. "Thanks, but no thanks, Portagee. We'll stick to the jungle trail. Your way will have us going through water, dense brush, and probably poison ivy."

Michael added, "Yeah, I think the trail will do."

Keno added, "I know where we're going. Follow me."

Graham smiled and said, "After you, big man."

Keno waved his arm for the group to follow him and went down the trail. One after another, the others followed him.

Meanwhile miles below the surface of Bermuda in Undercroft, Styx was meeting with his henchmen. He looked at his men and said, "Our time has come. Today my spies tell me that the princess will be in the Great Crystal Hall as they realign the crystal pendulum. We can kidnap the princess and destroy the crystal pendulum."

One of his henchmen replied, "What good does that do if we can't gain access to Atlantis?"

Styx reached across the table and backhanded the man across the room. He stood up and stared down at him and said, "You question me once more, and I'll feed you to the volcano. One of our dark beasts has managed to burrow deep under a crystal wall. Now all we have to do is break through the final foot or two." He looked over to his right and yelled, "Blackie, my pet, come here!"

Out of the shadows stepped a large, furry black beast with long, sharp fanged teeth and claws and a tail almost as long as the body of the beast. All of the henchmen stepped back out of fear for their lives.

As the beast neared Styx, he said, "Yes, master, the tunnel is ready. When do we go?"

Styx smiled as he rubbed Blackie's fur and said, "Go get some of your friends and meet us at the dig site in two hours." Blackie snarled and left the room.

Styx turned to his men and added, "Go pick twenty of your best warriors. This morning we capture the princess." His men were gone in seconds.

Chapter 3
The Invasion

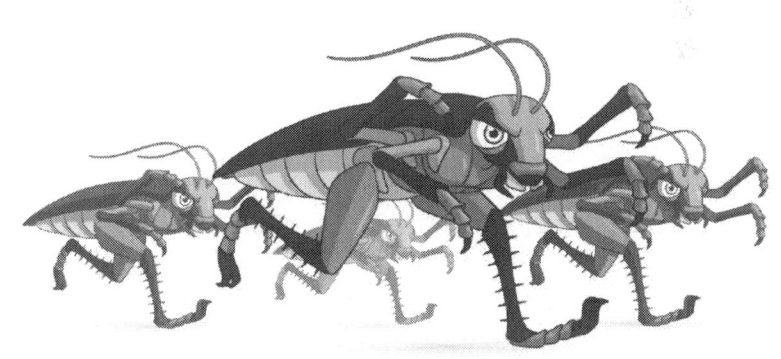

The Invasion

It was another beautiful day in Atlantis, but then every day in Atlantis is always the same. In this static environment, there is never a change from temperature to light of day. During "times of rest," which the Atlanteans say since they have no concept of night, shades are pulled to make the rooms dark.

Princess Ariadne was up early this morning. Today she was going to the Great Crystal Hall and then to the outer rim of Atlantis to spend time with some of her animal friends.

While the princess was on her way to the Great Crystal Hall, Styx and his band had already broken through the tunnel Blackie had dug. They quickly made their way toward the Great Crystal Hall to destroy the crystal pendulum.

Just as the Dredge and the beasts were entering the Great Crystal Hall, one of the patrolling sentries discovered the tunnel. He quickly sounded the alarm.

Back on the surface, the Spinners had finally made their way to the rocky area of the jungle, where they had hopes of spotting some skinks. They had already spread out to cover more ground.

After a while, Michael said with a little frustration in his voice, "Are you guys sure we're not on a snipe hunt?"

Sam snapped back, "Don't be such a baby. We're going to find some sooner or later."

Michael replied, "Yeah, later."

A few seconds later, Portagee yelled out, "I just saw one go into that cave over there!" He quickly ran in after it. One after another, the rest of the Spinners followed Portagee.

Once inside the cave, Graham said, "I can't see anything, much less a skink."

Keno added, "Just wait for a few minutes; your eyes will adjust to the dark." Shortly after that they were crawling around the cave floor and trying to find the elusive skink.

Back below the surface, Styx and his band were now in the Great Crystal Hall. They quickly made their way to the crystal pendulum. Styx yelled at the beast, "Destroy the pendulum!" Styx believed that if they destroyed the pendulum, Atlantis would be destroyed.

The beasts all leaped at the crystal pendulum, which caused it to spin out of control. Within seconds, the ground started shaking, and a mini earthquake began. The crystal pendulum broke off its mount, crashed to the ground, and broke into a thousand pieces.

In the middle of the earthquake, Princess Ariadne entered the Great Crystal Hall. To her horror, she saw that the beasts had destroyed the pendulum. Then she saw Styx and his henchmen.

At the same moment, Styx saw the princess and yelled to his men, "There's the princess; capture her!"

The captain of the guard was with the princess today. He signaled her escort to defend the princess. They were quickly overwhelmed.

The mortally wounded captain of the guard turned to one of the sentries and yelled, "Save the princess!" The young sentry and the princess made a hasty escape.

With the earthquake shaking the city, there was chaos in the streets. It was not long before Styx and his raiding party left the Great Crystal Hall with the beast tracking the princess. The princess and the sentry raced toward the outer rim, where they thought they could hide until the quake ended and the Dredge left the city.

Back on the surface, the Spinners were still in the cave when the earthquake began violently shaking the ground.

Sam screamed out, "Get out of the cave!"

But it was too late. As the entrance to the cave collapsed, the floor of the cave gave away. The Spinners found themselves sliding down what appeared to be an old air shaft. Because the shaft was in a diagonal pitch, they soon were able to regain their composure and hold on to each other as they descended into the earth.

It was like a never-ending slide ride. The Spinners kept their legs spread out and used their feet to scrape against the edge of the shaft in an attempt to slow down their speed. All of them feared what was waiting for them at the end of the ride: a sheer drop at some point or stalagmites from a cave floor. The only thing they were sure of was that there would be no pillow or cushion waiting for them.

Meanwhile, with all the chaos going on in the streets of Atlantis, the sentry and Princess Ariadne had made it to the outer rim, where they hoped it would be safe. Princess Ariadne sat down on a large stone to catch her breath and rest. Although the sentry was tired, he stood on guard while the princess rested.

Princess Ariadne looked over at the sentry and said, "Thank you so much for saving my life. What is your name, sentry?"

The sentry turned toward Princess Ariadne and said, "Pello." He was very young for a sentry and had just received his training. Although he was not a big man he was smart, quick and agile. Not to mention very handsome. Before he could say another word, they heard a massive crash in a cavern next to them.

The crash was the Spinners hitting the bottom of the shaft. After the crash, all that could be heard were some low-toned groans.

Keno was the first to speak up. "Is everyone OK?"

Graham replied, "How would I know? It's pitch black here. This time I really don't think my eyes are going to adjust to this darkness."

Michael stepped in. "Sam and Portagee, are you guys all right?"

Sam snapped back, "Yeah, but I'm not a guy."

In a panicked tone of voice, Portagee said, "I lost all my stuff. I can't find anything."

Graham added, "Welcome to my world, mate."

Out of nowhere on the other side of the cavern, a beam cast a light on the wall. A man wearing Greek military armor stepped into the light.

Michael looked up at the man and said, "Holy smokes, that guy is over twenty feet tall."

The Greek pulled his short sword out of its scabbard and pointed it at the Spinners. In a loud voice, he asked, "Why are you here? Are you part of the Dredge invasion?"

Sam stood up and stepped forward. She replied, "An earthquake caused us to fall down that open shaft over there."

The Greek asked, "Are you from the surface world?"

Sam replied, "Yes, and all we want is to get out of this pit."

The Greek held out his other hand; it had a round crystal in it. He added, "All of you step forward. I have something for you."

Keno yelled out, "Oh, no. Beware Greeks bearing gifts!"

The Greek yelled out, "Do it now, or I will crush you all!"

One after another, the Spinners lined up side by side. The Greek smiled and said, "That's better."

He pointed the crystal at the Spinners and cast a wavy, pulsating light at them. In seconds, they were overwhelmed by the light, and one after another, they lost consciousness. A few minutes later, they awoke.

Portagee looked up at the Greek and yelled out, "Look! He's over one hundred feet tall now."

A few seconds later, the Greek stepped out of the light, and to their amazement, he was really the same height as the Spinners.

Keno asked, "Why did you try to scare us and make us think you were a giant?"

The Greek replied, "We have just been attacked, and I had to make sure you were not part of the Dredge invaders."

Sam asked, "Why would you be worried about us? We thought you were three times our size."

The Greek smiled and replied, "That was all just an illusion. You were actually one hundred times my size."

Michael was confused, "We're the same size. What did you mean we were one hundred times your size?"

The Greek held out the crystal again and said, "With this crystal, I reduced you to my actual height. You're now about two inches tall."

The Spinners were stunned, and at first they didn't believe it. But as they looked around the cavern, they had to accept that it was true.

Graham asked, "Why did you do this to us?"

Princess Ariadne stepped out of the shadows and said, "You would have been trapped in this cavern and died here. Now you can leave with us."

Michael walked over to her and asked, "Other than getting out of this cavern, why would you want to be this size?"

Princess Ariadne ignored Michael's question and went on to say, "I am Princess Ariadne. Even though these may be bad circumstances, I want to welcome you to Atlantis."

The Spinners were all speechless.

After a short pause, the princess went on to say, "Thousands of years ago when my ancestors were trapped here beneath the sea, they also used the crystals to shrink themselves so that they could survive. Being small, they could go anywhere in the underworld, and they could live on a fraction of the food supply needed to feed the city."

Keno asked, "You mean there are more of you here?"

Princess Ariadne answered, "Yes, there are two kingdoms here beneath the sea." She went on and told them the story of the Dredge and the Atlanteans.

When she finished, Princess Ariadne turned to Pello and said, "This is Pello. He's one of my sentries, and he saved my life today. We fled the city, and I have no way of knowing if my sentries repelled the Dredge and their beasts or not."

Portagee asked, "What do you mean by beasts?"

Pello spoke up. "These beasts find their way here from your world.

Sam added, "There are no beasts in Bermuda."

Pello replied, "Yes, there are. You call them rats."

Sam replied, "Oh, great! I'm scared to death of rats, much less monster rats."

Michael stepped forward and said, "Don't worry, Sam. We're all here to protect you."

Princess Ariadne turned to the others and said, "It's time to leave. Follow me."

She turned and walked through a small crack in the cavern wall. Without saying another word, the Spinners followed.

Chapter 4
The City of Atlantis

The City of Atlantis

A short time later, as the small group was walking along, a dark, slimy creature slithered out from behind some rocks. Keno jumped back and yelled, "Holy smokes! It's an alligator."

Princess Ariadne laughed as she reached up to pet the creature and said, "This is my good friend Slink the skink."

Slink turned toward the Spinners and nodded his head and said, "Slink says, good day; I am Slink." The Spinners were stunned that a skink could talk.

Sam replied, "My, Slink, you have a different way of speaking." She walked over and patted him on the head.

Portagee asked, "Are you from the surface?"

Slink replied, "Slink says no. Two hundred years ago, many skinks left the surface of your world because it was much safer for us down here in this world."

Graham replied, "You chose wisely. You're an endangered species on the surface."

Slink turned back to the princess and said, "Slink says, there are many beasts in the area. I fear for your safety."

Princess Ariadne replied, "Pello will lead us home safely. You are welcome to follow us to the gates of the city."

Slink replied, "Slink says, as you wish." Although the skinks were allies of the Atlanteans, they never entered the city. They preferred to stay in the outer-rim area.

Once back in the city, Princess Ariadne and the Spinners were relieved to find that the Dredge had left the Great Crystal Hall and the city was secure again. However, the Dredge had accomplished their goal and destroyed the crystal pendulum.

The Spinners were amazed as they entered the city of Atlantis. This miniature city was breathtaking. As the princess and the Spinners made their way through the city, the constant tremors were a reminder that all was not well.

As soon as the princess was confident that the sentries were patrolling the city streets again, she and Pello took the Spinners on a tour of Atlantis. The Spinners were amazed at the Greek architecture throughout the city. Nothing was made out of marble or stone, as you would imagine it would be. Instead the columns, arches, and buildings were made out of coral and crystal. The pink coral and the clear crystals made the lost city radiant and beautiful. There was truly no place on earth like it.

In the center of Atlantis, the Spinners were surprised to find the most spacious fruit and vegetable garden one could imagine. As the Spinners walked through the garden, Sam turned to Princess Ariadne and said, "The center of the city is a strange place for a garden. I would have expected to find your palace here instead."

Princess Ariadne smiled and replied, "Our food source is the most precious resource we have in Atlantis. Without fruit and vegetables, we would be like the Dredge or die. Crystals and other jewels from our past are just that: objects from our past. With this garden in the center of the city, we can protect it and cultivate it. With the artificial light shining over the garden at all times, the fruit and vegetables grow much faster."

Portagee asked, "Have you ever tried to share your crops with the Dredge?"

Pello replied, "Every year after one of the harvests, we take baskets of surplus food to the outer rim for the Dredge, and they just let it rot. The rats and cockroaches end up eating it."

Michael patted him on the back and said, "Well, at least they can't say you haven't tried."

Keno said, "These crops are very different from what we grow on the surface."

Princess Ariadne replied, "These fruits and vegetables are from our ancestors and not from your world. They have been grown here for thousands of years, whereas yours crops have, for the most part, been introduced from other lands."

The small group left the garden and went on to the Great Crystal Hall. The inhabitants had secured the city from the Dredge attack, but the loss of life had been great. A group of sentries escorted the small group back to the Great Crystal Hall, where they viewed the damaged crystal pendulum.

Portagee walked up to the pendulum and asked, "What's wrong? I don't see anything missing."

Pello pointed to the shattered pendulum on the floor and said, "The Dredge have destroyed the pendulum, which holds our world in check. With that gone, your world and our world will soon begin feeling the effect of the upheaval. You know it as disruptions in the Bermuda Triangle, and it will be severe."

Michael asked, "So how are you going to replace it?"

Princess Ariadne replied, "We have not gone beyond the outer rim for over a thousand years. The Kingdom of Undercroft is a dark, treacherous place of no return, but we will have to go there to find another uncut crystal the size we need."

Sam asked, "Can you find one before it's too late?"

Princess Ariadne replied, "I can only hope so."

Pello added, "My princess, you know that the Dredge will try to stop us."

The princess hung her head and said, "Yes, I know."

The Spinners all looked at each other. They knew what had to be done. Graham spoke up first. "We will help you find a crystal and bring it back."

Pello walked over to the Spinners and said, "I will show you the way, my friends."

Princess Ariadne did not say a word. She walked out of the Great Crystal Hall and walked over to a bench overlooking a small saltwater lake that was fed by the ocean. She sat down and stared off into the distance.

Chapter 5
Captured

Captured

Unbeknown to the Spinners, a small party of creatures was closing in on the group. So far the Dredge had been successful. The crystal pendulum was now destroyed, and the Atlanteans would not be able to replace it without the help of Princess Ariadne.

Not long after that, the water in the lake began to churn out of control. As the princess stood up to move back from the waves crashing on the shore, a giant ghost crab surfaced from beneath the water. Moving sideways with his six legs, he left the water and grabbed the princess with his claws. The sentries fired arrows at the crab, but to no avail. The arrows just bounced off his hard shell. Seconds later he was back in the water with the princess.

As Pello and the Spinners rushed down to the water's edge, the ghost crab turned and said, "You fools cannot hurt me. I am the all-powerful Claws. Stay where you are, or I will snap her in two. She is now the prisoner of Styx and the Dredge." A second later Claws submerged with the princess and was gone.

Sam ran down to the shoreline. When Pello walked up next to her, she asked, "Is she going to drown?"

Pello replied, "No, we can hold our breath under water for over ten minutes. The ghost crab will take her to Styx and hold her captive. We must get some provisions and go quickly." Pello and the Spinners quickly made their way to gather provisions.

Back at Undercroft at the fortress of the Dredge, Styx received his gift from Claws. Styx walked over to the princess and said, "Your Majesty, after thousands of years of war, Atlantis has been finally defeated by a couple of raiding parties and a handful of crabs."

Ariadne snapped back, "You're nothing but a fool. By destroying the crystal, you have brought ruin to your own kingdom, too. Can't you feel the earth tremors here?"

Styx laughed and replied, "In our world of fire and brimstone, we have tremors all the time. These new tremors in Atlantis will surly shatter your crystal city."

Princess Ariadne more forcibly said, "You fool! The tremors are only the beginning. Soon there will be another upheaval that will devastate us all. The waters of the ocean will crash through our kingdoms and destroy us all."

Styx laughed again and said, "You would say anything now. When the coronation goes by without crowning a new queen, the dagger will be placed in the heart of Atlantis. Who knows? Maybe you'll become my queen." He looked at his men and added, "Take the princess to the dungeon and throw away the keys if she doesn't behave."

As Styx's thugs took Princess Ariadne away, she yelled out, "You just signed all our death warrants!"

Meanwhile back in Atlantis, Pello and the Spinners were ready to leave on their journey. The new captain of the guard met them with a small regiment of sentries. He stopped Pello and said, "Take these men with you to find the princess."

Pello replied, "Thank you, sir, but the Dredge will not be expecting a small group. We have not stepped foot in their lands for an eternity. With the sentries, they will see us coming and might do harm to the princess."

The captain nodded his head and said, "I will give you six high tides in the lake. If you have not returned by then, I will send sentries after you."

Pello saluted the captain and replied, "Yes, sir." He turned and waved the Spinners to follow him.

Once outside the city and into the outer rim, they were met by a surprise visitor. It was Slink the skink with a friend.

Portagee walked over to Slink and asked, "Slink, who's your friend? He looks familiar."

Slink replied, "Slink says, he should. He's Weezer, the tree frog. We call him Weezer because he can't sing like other tree frogs. All he can make are wheezing sounds when he tries to sing."

Although tree frogs are very tiny in the surface world, compared to the size of the Spinners, he was the size of a small dog. Sam walked over and gave him a pat on the head.

Weezer jumped up into Sam's arms and began trying to sing like tree frogs do on the surface. Sam could not believe how terrible the sound was. Trying to get him to stop singing, she asked, "Do you talk?"

Weezer quit his awful singing and replied, "Maybe." He leaped out of Sam's arms and onto Slink's back.

Slink yelled out, "Slink says, let's go!"

Pello said, "Slink, you're not a tracker. How can you help?"

Slink replied, "Slink says, they don't call me Slink the Sneak for nothing. I'll sneak around and warn you of danger. If I'm too far away, Weezer will let out a little song for you to hear."

Pello replied, "So be it. Off with you." Slink quietly slithered off with Weezer on his back.

As they were about to leave the rim, Pello stopped and looked at the tunnel they were going to have to walk through. Michael walked up next to him and asked, "Is there a problem?"

Pello replied, "Not really, I've just never been beyond this spot in my entire life. Going into the dark-dwellers' territory has always been forbidden."

Keno slapped Pello on the back and said, "Well, mate, not anymore. After all, what else could eat us besides giant crabs and rats?"

Portagee stepped up and asked, "Do you have cockroaches down here? They're already monstrous in Bermuda. I can't imagine how big they would be down here."

Pello didn't answer. He pulled out his short Greek sword and walked into the tunnel. All of the Spinners took Pello's lead and pulled out their swords and followed Pello into the tunnel.

The tunnel itself was not very large and must have been about a quarter of a mile long by Atlantean standards. Once they exited the tunnel, it was a night-and-day difference between the two worlds. The group stopped to gaze at the kingdom of Undercroft.

The Spinners all felt like they had just stepped into a volcano. There was black smoke everywhere. Small fires were burning out of cracks in the rocks everywhere. These fires were burning from low-grade natural-gas deposits in the ground.

The razor-sharp, jagged rocks and boulders everywhere made the Spinners feel like they were on a distant planet in another galaxy. There was also a massive lake in the cavern, with fire burning on the surface of it. The water of the lake was as black as coal. It had been contaminated over the years by the state of Undercroft.

Sam stood there and held her sword. All of a sudden, she felt very awkward holding the sword. She slid it back into her scabbard and said, "I don't know what I'm doing with a sword. I'm never going to use it."

Michael walked up to her and said, "Don't ever say 'never,' but just in case, keep that sword close to you."

Pello looked down at the cavern floor and found some tracks. He looked at the others and said, "These tracks are fairly fresh. Let's move out and see where they lead us."

Undercroft was uncharted land as far as Pello was concerned. No Atlantean had stepped foot in these lands for ages. Pello led the way, with the Spinners following in single file after him. At least for the time being, the tracks appeared to be going along the lake's shoreline. The Spinners kept an eye on the water just in case another ghost crab was out there.

Later that afternoon while taking a rest stop, the Spinners were passing around a leather water bottle. Just before taking a sip, Pello said, "Conserve your water. Something tells me that it might be in short supply in this devil's hole."

Sam looked around at the landscape of Undercroft. She looked at Pello and asked, "Do the Atlanteans feel any remorse for forcing the Dredge to live in a world like this?"

Pello paused for a moment and replied, "I suppose so; however, the Dredge did try to slaughter my people in the rebel war. Although this kingdom has always been volcanic, it has not always been this harsh. The Dredge are a people who are determined to kill anything green and living. They suck the life out of the living with no concern for conservation. They are content with living off mushrooms, mold, bugs, and who knows what else. It is sad, but they control their own destiny."

Michael nudged Sam in the side and said, "Don't feel sorry for them when they command one of those giant rats to attack us."

Sam snapped back, "Shut up!"

Graham stood up and said, "Let's go, mates. Somewhere in the world, daylight is burning, and we're wasting time."

The small tracking party moved out. A short time later, Pello stopped the group. They had come to a fork in the path. Pello turned to the others and said, "The tracks stop dead here at the fork in the path. I don't have a clue which way they went."

Portagee spoke up, "It looks to me like they went one of three ways."

Keno interrupted him. "Whoa, little buddy, this fork only has two paths."

Portagee smiled and said, "True, but they could have gone in the water."

Graham looked out over the lake and said, "I'm not going out there. Did you guys see what kind of things float out there in the water?"

Sam looked and said, "Count me out, too. Those black, iridescent blobs are some type of floating Portuguese man-of-war fish. I bet they have one nasty sting."

Pello looked surprised; he had never seen a Portuguese man-of-war before. He then added, "I agree. Even if they went out in the water, we'll stay on firm ground."

Just then a tremor shook the ground and knocked them off their feet.

While they were getting back to their feet, a voice said, "Slink says, they went by water."

Michael asked, "Did you and Weezer see them?" He looked around and asked, "Where's Weezer?"

Slink replied, "Slink says, yes, we saw them. They climbed on the backs of ghost crabs and went off in that direction."

He pointed with his tail in the direction in which they had gone.

Sam spoke up and said, "So where's Weezer?"

Slink shook his head and replied, "Slink says, Weezer leaped on the back of one of the crabs without being seen. Now he can tell us where they went."

Pello asked, "So if we can't hear Weezer sing, how are we going to know where they are?"

Slink replied, "Slink says, I don't think Weezer thought of that. It did sound like a good idea at the time."

Sam replied, "Well, I hope nothing bad happens to Weezer."

Pello then said, "We better stay on the path next to the lake."

Slink and the group continued on the path that followed the lake's shoreline.

Chapter 6
Waterfall of Death

Waterfall of Death

It was much later in the day, or so they thought. After all, since they were underground, they never knew if it was day or night. The cavern wall almost touched the lake. As they drew closer to that point, a waterfall came into view. The source of the water flowed out of a jagged cave. It almost looked like the head of some type of alien being. Even the water that flowed from the cave was blackish.

Keno looked up at the waterfall and said, "I'm not getting thirsty looking at that water."

Portagee added, "Yeah, I'm not getting the urge to go swimming, either."

Sam, who was also looking at the waterfall, said, "I don't see a way of getting by this waterfall unless we backtrack and climb the mountain."

Michael added to the conversation. "I never met a waterfall where there wasn't a secret passage that you could walk through."

Graham added, "I'll bet he's right."

Sam looked at Pello and said, "These guys are insane."

Pello smiled and replied, "I think it's worth a try."

With a look that could kill, Sam said, "Oh, lord."

Pello looked over at Slink and asked, "Slink, are you going first?"

Slink replied, "Slink says no! Skinks don't like this water, either."

Pello turned toward the waterfall and said, "Follow me." He quickly disappeared into the waterfall.

Seconds later the Spinners heard a scream, and then a big lump flowed down the waterfall and disappeared into the mist below.

At first the Spinners stood there in silence. Finally, Michael said, "We've got to go in there and find Pello."

Graham added, "I hope he's in there. We'd better go now."

All of the Spinners pulled out their swords, except for Sam, and one behind the other, they followed Michael through the waterfall. Once inside, Keno looked down and saw blood on the floor. Keno pointed at it and said, "Pello ran into something and something, or someone got hurt."

Graham added, "It looks to me like both of them fell into the waterfall."

Michael said as he kept walking, "Let's get out of here and back out into the open air. We can talk once we get outside." Nothing else was said, and they all quickly walked along the narrow ledge under the waterfall.

Once outside, Portagee looked at the others and said, "Now what? We're on our own and don't know where we are going."

Before the other could speak, Slink said, "Slink says, follow me. My friends have been captured, and I need your help."

Sam walked over to Slink and gave him a hug around his neck and said, "Don't worry, Slink. We'll help you find your friends."

Slink's tail wagged. He gave Sam a lick on the face with his sticky tongue and said, "Slink says, thanks."

Sam wiped the sticky saliva from her face and replied, "You're welcome."

With swords drawn, they left the waterfall and stayed their course along the water's edge. Two hours later they found an area with boulders that they could hide behind and rest. Whether it was night or not, it didn't matter; the Spinners were all tired and needed a nap.

Keno stood up and said, "You all go to sleep, and I'll take the first watch. Portagee, you can take the second watch."

Sam lay down, and before she knew what had happened, Slink lay down next to her. She had acquired a new friend who was probably not going to leave her side.

A few minutes later, everyone but Keno was sound asleep. Tomorrow would bring another day.

Chapter 7
The Escape

The Escape

The next morning in Undercroft, Princess Ariadne was woken by a massive tremor that rocked the entire Dredge kingdom. By the time the tremor had ended and the dust settled, Princess Ariadne looked up to see that the dungeon door had been rocked off its hinges. She quickly got to her feet and ran out the door. To her surprise, once she was out the door, she heard a tiny voice say, "Princess, follow me; I will help you escape."

Princess Ariadne looked down and was shocked to see Weezer. She said, "Weezer, my dear, look at you. This climate is not good for your skin." She was right; Weezer's skin was drying up from the added heat and smoke in Undercroft.

Weezer leaped up into her arms and replied, "Don't worry, Princess. There're lots of small water holes along the way that I can soak in." He leaped back down to the ground and said, "Not a moment to lose, Princess. We need to get out of here before the Dredge discover you're missing."

Princess Ariadne nodded her head and said, "You lead the way, and I'll follow." Weezer hopped down the passageway, with the princess right behind him.

Meanwhile back at the Spinners' camp, Graham was slowly waking up. Still groggy, he was having trouble making out something that appeared to be watching him from a rock not far away. After a minute, he could tell what it was. He jumped up and yelled, as he pulled out his sword, "Look! It's a giant cockroach!"

The cockroach was standing on the rock and was about the size of a wolf compared to the Spinners' current size.

The rest of the Spinners were now awake. Keno spoke up first, "There's only one. We can handle the cockroach."

Slink added, "Slink says, there's never just one. They run in packs and look for defenseless or dead creatures." Just then six more cockroaches climbed up from behind the rock and joined their friend.

Sam's worse nightmare had just come true. As she stepped backward, she tripped and fell down. Instantly one of the cockroaches picked up on her fall and leaped off the rock at her. Sam screamed.

Michael leaped in front of her with his sword pulled out, but before he could do anything, Slink's long tongue shot out of his mouth like a rocket and snapped the cockroach in midair and back into his mouth in a second.

Slink smiled and said, "Slink says, Slink likes cockroaches." The rest of the cockroaches quickly vanished.

As Michael helped Sam back to her feet, she looked at Slink and said, "Don't you dare lick me with that tongue ever again." She walked over to Slink and gave him a hug and said, "Thanks for saving me."

Portagee looked at the others and said, "Holy smokes, those creepy bugs are lightning fast. We need to find the princess and a crystal and get out of here."

Graham looked at Slink and asked, "What now, Slink? Which way should we go?"

Slink looked out across the lake and said, "Slink says, we should go over the water."

Portagee replied, "No way am I swimming out there with those big blobs waiting to sting me."

Slink smiled and waddled over to the lake and turned around and began slapping his tail in the water.

Michael whispered to Sam, "What's he doing? Is he trying to scare the man-of-war's away?"

Sam replied, "Not a clue, but I'm sure we'll find out soon."

A few minutes later, Slink stopped splashing his tail and returned back to where the Spinners were standing. He turned back around, and without saying a word, he stared at the black lake.

Another ten minutes passed, and then out of nowhere, a large island rose out of the lake. Amazed, the Spinners stepped backward, while Slink ran down to the lakeshore.

Keno looked at the others with a puzzled face and said, "What's going on?"

A second later they got their answer. A very large head popped out of the water. The Spinners could now see that it was not an island they were looking at; instead, it was an enormous sea turtle. The turtle slowly swam over to the shoreline where Slink was waiting.

Slink yelled back to the Spinners, "Slink says, come meet my friend."

The Spinners walked down to the lakeshore. Slink pointed his tail back and forth between the Spinners and the sea turtle and said, "Slink says, this is my good friend Snorkel the sea turtle. Snorkel, these are my new friends from the surface. They call themselves the Spinners."

Snorkel looked a little puzzled. He said, "You should be bigger than me. How come you're so small like the Atlanteans?"

Sam stepped forward and replied, "It's a long story, but to make it short, the Atlanteans shrunk us because we were trapped in a cave."

Slink walked closer to Snorkel and said, "Slink says, we need passage across the lake. Can you help?"

Snorkel smiled and replied, "I would be glad to take you, but should you slip off my shell into the black lake, the creatures with the tentacles may sting you to death."

Michael asked, "Aren't you afraid that you will get stung?"

Snorkel replied, "Naw, my old shell and hide are so thick that they can't hurt me even if they try."

Slink jumped on Snorkel's head and then onto his shell. With his tail, he waved to the others and said, "Slink says, follow me; it's time to go."

Snorkel placed his head down on the sand, and one after another, the Spinners carefully stepped on his nose and then to his head and climbed onto his shell.

Once everyone was aboard, Snorkel used his massive front flappers to shove off from the shoreline. Slowly he turned around in the water and began swimming across the lake.

Chapter 8
The Black Lake

The Black Lake

The Black Lake was a dangerous place. Not even the Dredge would go out on it unless on the backs of the ghost crabs. While Snorkel slowly moved along, the Spinners were on a constant lookout for Portuguese man-of-war's and crabs. Both of these creatures could end their lives in seconds.

The ride was slow and eerie. Not only did they feel like they were in another world, but they also knew that if something went wrong and they ended up in the lake, it would probably be the end of their journey.

On the other hand, Slink was constantly running around them like he was on a joy ride. He kept chattering to Snorkel like he was his long-lost friend. Every so often Snorkel would drop his head beneath the water. The Spinners could not tell if he was making sure he was not being followed or he was tired of listening to Slink.

About halfway across the lake, another upheaval struck. Graham pointed to the roof of the cavern and yelled out, "Look out! Pieces of the roof of the cavern are breaking loose!"

Seconds later huge chunks of the roof began falling in the water all around them. One of the chunks struck the shell of Snorkel, causing him to roll to one side. The Spinners tried to grab on to anything they could. Slink quickly wrapped his tail around Sam and saved her while Michael grabbed hold of one of his legs.

The suction power on Slink's feet allowed him to stay on Snorkel's back without moving. Portagee and Graham slid down the shell and landed on Snorkel's head. Keno was not so lucky. He slid off the side of Snorkel's shell and splashed into the lake.

At first Keno was very calm in the water and began swimming toward Snorkel. Suddenly out of nowhere, a large spike surfaced from beneath the water.

Portagee yelled out, "Keno! Look out! There's something behind you."

By the time Keno had turned around, the creature was in full view. Sam screamed, "It's a lionfish! Get out of the water!"

Sam was right. Lionfish in the surface world are one of the most destructive fish in the ocean. Their prey is small fish that swim in shallow coral reefs. They can quickly destroy the balance of nature in these areas of the ocean.

Because of the large poisonous spikes protruding from their bodies, they have few predatory enemies in the ocean. In recent years, the Dredge had learned to use their poisonous spikes as spears. The two-inch miniature inhabitants of these subterranean caves were a tasty morsel for the lionfish.

Slink was at a loss as to what to do. All he could say was, "Slink says, what to do? What to do?"

The lionfish was closing in fast on Keno. He was never going to make it back to Snorkel in time. The lionfish's mouth was now wide open. He was going to swallow Keno in one gulp.

Michael let go of Slink and jumped to his feet. He ran and leaped as high as he could and shot himself like a projectile at the lionfish. In the middle of the leap, he yelled out, "Geronimo!"

In midair, Michael pulled out his sword. Just at the point of impact in the water between Keno and the lionfish, Michael jammed his sword in the lionfish's mouth and forced it wide open. The lionfish shook his head in an attempt to dislodge the sword, but to no avail.

As Michael and Keno were swimming back toward Snorkel, the lionfish flipped on his side and caused one of his poisonous spikes to scratch Michael. The lionfish then disappeared beneath the surface of the water.

Once the two boys were close to Snorkel, he turned his head in their direction and lowered his head down into the water so that they could climb on his head and back onto his shell. The other Spinners helped Keno and Michael back to the center area of Snorkel's shell. As

Sam grabbed Michael's right arm to pull him up, Michael let out a big yelp.

Sam looked at his arm and asked, "What happened to your arm? You've got a large scratch on it; you're bleeding."

Michael looked at his arm and said, "It's nothing; that big, dumb fish scratched me."

Portagee jumped up and quickly pulled off his belt and strapped it around Michael's arm like a tourniquet. He yelled out, "We have to stop that poison quickly!"

Portagee was right. The poison that had been released into Michael would paralyze him very quickly. Portagee hoped that he could treat Michael like he had received a snakebite. He began trying to suck the poison out of Michael's arm with his mouth and spit it out.

Portagee's treatment worked for the most part; however, Michael's arm did go limp, and he could not move it. Fortunately for Michael, the poison did not get into his blood stream and reach his heart.

With his right arm limp, Michael rested his left arm on Portagee's shoulder and said, "Thanks, buddy. I think you just saved my life."

Portagee started to reply, but all that came out of his mouth were some slurred words that didn't make any sense.

Graham laughed and said, "Well, mate, I think that poison you sucked into your mouth made it go numb. Just like getting a shot at the dentist."

Sam looked over at Portagee and said, "Don't worry; you'll be talking soon."

Keno added, "Yeah, but quit drooling like a baby."

Portagee gave Keno a big shove and then gave him a high five. The tremors over and the lionfish gone, Snorkel continued swimming.

Another two hours went by before they were closing in on the opposite shoreline of the lake. As Snorkel paddled his way up to the shore, they could only believe that they were jumping from the frying pan into the fire. The shoreline was lined with cliffs that might as well have been a mile high in comparison to their two-inch size.

One after another, the Spinners and Slink slid down Snorkel's shell and landed on the beach. Each one of the Spinners thanked Snorkel. As they walked toward the cliffs, Snorkel said, "Don't forget; if you need me, just splash."

Slink replied, "Slink says, we will."

Snorkel waved good-bye with one of his flippers. He shoved off from the beach and submerged himself beneath the water.

Chapter 9
The Labyrinth

The Labyrinth

The tunnel Weezer had used to find Princess Ariadne had collapsed in the upheaval. So now they found themselves lost in the endless tunnels of the Undercroft labyrinth with very little chance of escape.

Meanwhile the Dredge henchmen had discovered the escape of Princess Ariadne. Two of the henchman found Styx feasting on bugs and mushrooms in the king's chamber. The first henchman yelled out, "The princess has escaped!"

Styx spat out his food, jumped up, and yelled, "How in Hades did she get away?"

The henchman replied, "The tremor shook the cell door off its hinges."

Styx grabbed him by the throat and said, "Call out the cockroaches and rats. She can't be far."

The two henchmen ran out of the room. Styx smashed his fist down on the table, causing it to shatter into a million pieces. He stood up and kicked the chair he had been sitting on across the room. He stomped out of the room and looked for his men.

Once outside, he found Blackie waiting for him. Styx told him, "Take your brothers with you and a pack of cockroaches. Track the princess down and bring her back to me. Some of my men will follow."

Blackie snarled as he looked at the cockroaches and said, "Track her." The pack of cockroaches left in a heartbeat, with the three rats close behind them.

It wasn't long before the long antennae of the cockroaches picked up the trail of the princess in the labyrinth. They quickly moved out, with Blackie and the other rats not far behind. The twitching of the cockroaches' antennae resonated throughout the labyrinth.

The princess was not able to pick up on the sound, but Weezer's sharp hearing did. Weezer stopped hopping and turned back and looked at the princess. The princess looked down at Weezer and asked, "Weezer, what is it? Why did we stop?"

Weezer replied, "I can hear the cockroaches, and they're tracking us. It won't be long before they catch up to us if we don't lose them somehow. We need to start moving much faster."

The princess didn't say a word. She started running and motioned to Weezer to catch up to her. Weezer began hopping as fast as he could. A short time later, they came up to another dead end, where the tunnel had also collapsed from the upheaval.

Both stopped and stared at the collapsed wall for a minute. Finally, the princess pointed to the floor and said, "Look, Weezer. There's a small opening in the dirt."

Weezer leaped over to the opening and began digging as fast as he could. The princess yelled out, "Hurry, Weezer! I can hear them coming."

Seconds later Weezer broke through into the adjoining tunnel. He looked back at the princess to let her know. Then he saw the cockroaches closing in on her.

The princess yelled, "It's too late! Go find the others." Without saying another word, Princess Ariadne waved a crystal at the tunnel causing it to collapse. Before she could say another word, the cockroaches were climbing all over her. She screamed in terror as she swatted at them.

Suddenly there was a loud screech. The cockroaches instantly jumped off the princess and went running back down the tunnel.

When the princess regained her composure, she was looking at Blackie and his two sidekicks. She took a swing at Blackie, but before she could connect with her fist, Blackie slapped her upside her head with his lethal tail. Princess Ariadne was knocked unconscious.

Blackie looked at the other two rats and said, "Take her back to Styx." The two rats picked the princess up and headed back to the Dredge fortress.

On the other side of the collapsed tunnel, Weezer heard what happened. He knew that the Princess Ariadne was all right. He would now need help from Pello and the Spinners. Hoping to find them, he hopped off.

Chapter 10
A Lost Friend

A Lost Friend

Meanwhile the Spinners were standing at the base of the cliffs, staring up, not knowing what to do. Then from behind them, they heard a voice. "Thanks for waiting for me. I didn't know when I was going to catch up to you."

To the shock of the Spinners, it was Pello. He looked a bit roughed up but nonetheless in pretty good shape. Sam ran over to Pello, gave him a hug, and asked, "What happened to you? We lost you in the waterfall."

Pello smiled and replied, "I lost my footing on the wet rocks behind the waterfall and slipped off the edge. Almost the second I hit the water below, a lionfish gulped me down for his lunch."

Graham asked, "How in the heck did you survive?"

Pello replied, "I was very lucky. In the fall, I managed to hang on to my sword. After about thirty seconds, I realized where I was. I started hacking at the gills of the lionfish. It wasn't long before he floated to the surface, and then I climbed out through the hole I had created in his gills. Finally, he floated up on this beach where I could jump off and cut off a couple of his spikes. I thought they might come in handy if I ran into any monster rats."

Michael added, "Believe me, we're glad to have you back." He pointed to Sam and said, "Why don't you give one of those spears to Sam? She has nothing to defend herself with."

Pello handed her one of the spears. Sam replied, "Oh, that's great. Now I can poison myself."

Keno, still looking up at the cliffs, said, "Do we really have to go up there?"

Pello replied, "Step back, closer to the shoreline, take another look, and tell me what you see."

Pello and the Spinners all backed up about twenty-five feet and looked up again. Portagee yelled out, "Holy smokes! It looks like a skull in the side of the cliff."

Pello replied, "Yes, I've heard stories about Skull Mountain before, but I thought it was just fantasy."

Michael added, "Well, guess what? They're true! So tell us the story about Skull Mountain."

Pello was slow to continue, but finally he did. "Skull Mountain is the true gateway to the Dredge kingdom."

Graham interrupted him. "What the heck is all this? I feel like we've already been through Disneyworld."

Pello looked confused. Sam poked Graham in the ribs and said, "Pello, don't pay any attention to him. Please go on with your story."

Pello nodded and went on to say, "Well, there's really not much to tell. To my knowledge, no Atlanteans have ever returned from Skull Mountain."

Keno spoke up. "So you're saying that in thousands of years, no one has ever made it back from Skull Mountain, and we're about to enter the skull?"

Pello replied, "Yes, that is, if we can find our way up the cliff just to get to the skull entrance."

Portagee said, "Well, daylight's burning somewhere. Let's get going."

Pello added, "Follow me." One after another, the Spinners followed Pello as he began to climb the jagged rocks up the side of the cliff.

After about twenty minutes of climbing, Michael turned and looked back at Sam and said, "I can't believe this is the way the Dredge climb this cliff every time. There must be a simpler way."

Just then Portagee yelled out, "Look over to your right! It looks like a small tunnel hidden by the rocks."

The group made their way over to the tunnel. It appeared to be a passageway that might lead them up to the skull entrance.

Slink had been very quiet for quite some time. He looked at the others and said, "Slink says, I'll go up the tunnel first, and you can follow." Before anyone could answer, Slink was gone.

Pello pulled out his sword and went into the tunnel after Slink. Michael looked at the other Spinners and said, "Let's do this." The rest of the Spinners followed Michael into the tunnel.

The tunnel was only about three inches high, so the Spinners hoped that the rats would not be in there. The tunnel made for a very steep and winding climb up the cliff. There were hundreds of stairs that had been cut into the rough stone in the tunnel; the Spinners knew that this must be taking them to the entrance to the skull. Every so often they would come across what appeared to be open windows looking out over the vast lake.

It seemed to take hours as the small group made its way up the winding stairs. No one had heard from Slink since he had entered the tunnel. Then all of a sudden, Slink came running down the stairs at full speed. He screamed out, "Slink says, run for your lives! A rat is chasing me."

As Slink ran past the Spinners, they looked back up the tunnel. All they could see was that the tunnel was going black in color. Finally, they figured out why.

Sam yelled, "Look! That rat is completely filling up the tunnel." The group would have to run back down the tunnel or jump out of the closest window.

Pello knew that neither option was going to work. The rat would rip them to shreds in seconds. Pello yelled, "Graham and Sam, get up here quickly with your spears. Michael and Keno, back them up."

Graham and Sam knelt down on one knee and pointed the tips of their spears in the direction of the rat. Michael and Keno leaned on their backs, which gave them support and braced them for the clash with the rat. The rat was so consumed with attacking the Spinners that he never slowed down. The rat hit the spears at full speed, which sent the Spinners and Pello rolling head over heels back down the tunnel.

As the dust settled, everyone appeared to be unscathed. Slink ran back to the group and said, "Slink says, I'm sorry I did not stay and fight."

Sam reached over and gave him a hug and said, "You warned us and saved us all. Thank you."

Slink gave her a lick on her face with his sticky tongue. Sam cringed and said, "Thanks, but you don't have to do that."

Portagee walked up to the dead rat and said, "How in the heck are we going to get around this giant dead rat? He's completely clogged the tunnel."

Keno walked up and pulled out his sword and said, "I know one way."

Sam walked up from behind Keno and gave him a small shove and said, "That's not going to happen. There must be some other way."

Michael stepped in and added, "He's just kidding, Sam. We've got to pull the rat back down the tunnel to a window opening and shove him out of it."

Pello and the Spinners all tried to pull the dead rat down the tunnel, but that proved to be impossible. He was now lodged tightly in the tunnel.

Pello looked at the others and said, "Let's take a break."

Chapter 11
Skull Mountain

Skull Mountain

A short time later, Pello stood up and said, "The only way to go up is to go down."

The Spinners all knew what he meant. They would now have to go back down to the beach and find another way up the cliff. Ten minutes later they came across Slink lying down in front of one of the tunnel windows.

Sam looked at him and said, "Slink, thanks for waiting for us."

Slink replied, "Slink says, you're welcome, Sam. I have been waiting to show you another way up to the top of Skull Mountain."

Graham looked out the window and said, "That's easy for you to say. You can climb upside down."

Slink added, "Slink says, just follow me. I can get you up to the next window on the other side of the rat." With that, he slithered out the window. About ten feet up the side of the cliff, he stopped and said, "Slink says, I'm waiting. Follow me; you'll be safe."

Michael looked out the window and up at Slink and said, "Oh, yeah, I've heard that before. Climb out a window the equivalent of a couple of thousand feet off the ground."

Sam asked, "So does that mean you're not going out there?"

Michael replied, "Heck, no. Count me in." He stood out on the ledge and held his hand out to Sam and asked, "Are you coming?"

Sam took his hand and climbed out on the ledge and said, "Just promise me you won't let me look down."

Michael replied, "You got it." Michael and Sam slowly climbed their way up the cliff to where Slink was waiting. Pello and the other Spinners followed behind them.

A fall from this height would be instant death. They didn't dare to look down as they slowly made their ascent higher and higher up Skull Mountain. Slink slithered his way in and out of the rocks and made the climb look simple. For Pello and the Spinners, it was anything but that.

Portagee and Keno were bringing up the rear. Keno knew that he was the biggest by far. He feared that if he fell, he would take someone else with him. As Keno tried to keep up with the others, his worst fear happened. He slipped on a loose rock and started sliding down the cliff.

A quick-thinking Portagee spun his body around and grabbed Keno's arm with his right hand while at the same time he tried to dig his sandals into the rocks. Because

Keno was almost twice the size of Portagee, he was beginning to pull them both down the cliff. The problem was that they were only about ten feet from a ledge that would send them falling to their death.

Portagee yelled out, "Someone grab my legs!"

It was too late for the rest of the group. They were all too far away from them now to grab the boys before they fell. With Keno only a foot from the ledge, the others were still trying to get to them. All of a sudden, a long sticky rope tied itself around Portagee's waist and stopped the sliding process. Keno's feet were now hanging over the ledge.

Slink had shot out his tongue and wrapped it around Portagee and stopped the sliding. As a safety precaution, Slink had wrapped his tail around a rock. Sam scooted over to Slink and helped to hold him in place while Michael, Graham, and Pello quickly moved down the cliff to pull Keno and Portagee back to safe footing.

As they pulled the pair to safety, Keno said, "Thanks, mates. I was a goner for sure."

Portagee gave Keno a hug and said, "I would never let my best friend fall off a cliff."

Keno smiled and gave Portagee a hug back and said, "Little brother, it's the thought that counts."

Michael added, "Yeah, and it's really Slink who counts." He turned and gave Slink a pat on the head.

Slink turned around and said as he headed back up the cliff, "Slink says, it's nice to have friends."

After about twenty minutes, Slink found another window that he could crawl through. Ten minutes later the rest of the group made their way through the window.

Once everyone was back inside the tunnel, Pello said, "We're not far from the entrance to the skull. We will need to be careful; the Dredge may be waiting for us."

Sam added, "Just as long as their rats aren't there, waiting for us, too."

Slowly, one stair after another, they made their way up the tunnel. Graham commented, "This is the toughest hike I've ever gone on."

Michael asked, "Do you mean with or without the rat and the fall?" Graham was winded. He smiled and kept moving without saying another word.

Not long after that, they made their way to the entrance cave to Skull Mountain. It was just as eerie as anyone could imagine. The skull entrance appeared to be a natural formation in the face of the cliff.

Portagee looked at Keno and said, "How in the heck could something this evil looking be created by Mother Nature?"

Pello answered before Keno could. "Mother Nature had nothing to do with this. The demons from Hades did this."

Sam looked over at Michael and said, "Oh, this just keeps getting better."

Michael smiled and replied, "Right now I would rather go through the skull than back down that tunnel."

Sam took Michael's hand and squeezed it. Michael almost melted at the touch of her hand. Portagee interrupted the little moment by saying, "Come on; enough of this sweet stuff. Let's go get Princess Ariadne."

Pello pulled out his sword and said, "Follow me, my friends."

Before Pello could take his first step, Slink ran into the cave and was out of sight in seconds. One after another, the small rescue group walked through the mouth of the skull.

Chapter 12
Welcome to Hades

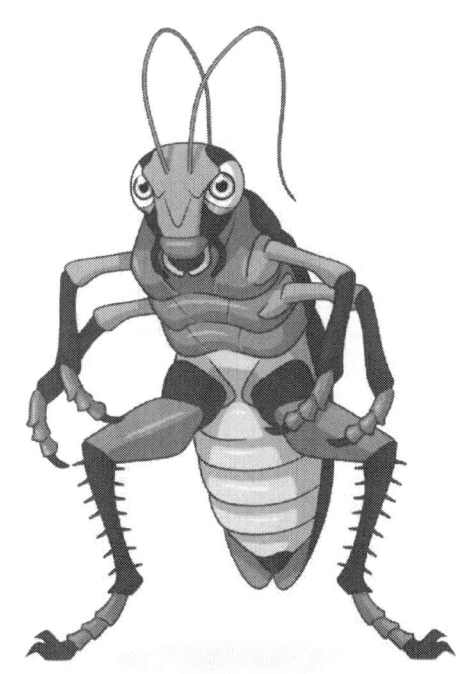

Welcome to Hades

Once they were inside the small cave, they saw that tunnels went in all directions. Pello stopped, looked in all directions, and tried to decide which way to go. Keno asked, "Should we split up and go into different tunnels?"

Graham snapped back, "Are you kidding me? If we split up, we'll never find each other, and who knows what's out there waiting for us."

Portagee kept staring at the different tunnels and finally said, "The tunnel in the center has a much smoother floor in it. That means that for years more creatures or people have used it to come and go through the skull. I think we should stay together and go down that tunnel. I bet Slink has already done so."

Pello looked at the others and said, "Follow me; the princess awaits us." One after another, the Spinners followed Pello down the center tunnel.

After about an hour of walking, Portagee said, "Boy, I hope they don't have miniature vampire bats down here."

Pello replied, "I have never seen a bat down here, but I have read about them in the surface world."

Sam added, "Well, at least that's good news."

As they walked along, Michael whispered to Pello, "I get the feeling we're being followed."

Pello whispered back, "We are; there's been a pack of cockroaches following us for the last thirty minutes."

Michael replied, "What should we be doing?"

Pello said, "Nothing. They're too fast for us to catch, not that you would want to. If they disappear, then we know that they went to tell the Dredge where we are. If they attack us, then we fight, but they usually only prey on dead or wounded creatures. However, if Slink were here, he might want to eat one."

Sam joined in on the conversation. "That's gross! Let's keep moving."

Not long after that, Slink returned to the group. Slink was licking his mouth. Pello looked at him and asked, "Did you have cockroaches for dinner, Slink?"

Slink smiled and said, "Slink says, oh, yes, they were very tasty. I left some parts farther down the tunnel if you want some."

Sam bent over and coughed a few times in an attempt not to get sick. Michael looked over at Pello and said, "Well, I guess the Dredge won't find out about us anytime soon, thanks to Slink."

81

An hour later they came out of the back side of the mountain. The landscape was darker and the air harder to breath because of all the smoking fires everywhere. Pello looked around and said, "Welcome to Hades. Yes, the inner land of Dredge would easily be considered to be Hades by anyone from the surface world."

Graham asked, "How can these two so-different worlds coexist next to each other for thousands of years?"

Just then another tremor struck and knocked them all off their feet. As Pello stood back up, he said, "Maybe they won't, unless we find Princess Ariadne and another crystal pendulum." Pello looked over at Slink and asked, "Slink, it looks like a vast area to search. Do you have any idea which way to go?"

Slink replied, "Slink says, I have picked up a scent of at least one rat. I can follow it."

Pello replied, "That's good, but have you picked up the scent of Princess Ariadne yet?"

Slink dropped his head and shook it from side to side. Pello rubbed his side and added, "That's OK. Let's move out."

Slink lifted up his head and ran down the side of the mountain toward the floor of the massive cavern. Pello waved at the others to follow as he went after Slink at a brisk walk.

Chapter 13
The Fortress of the Dredge

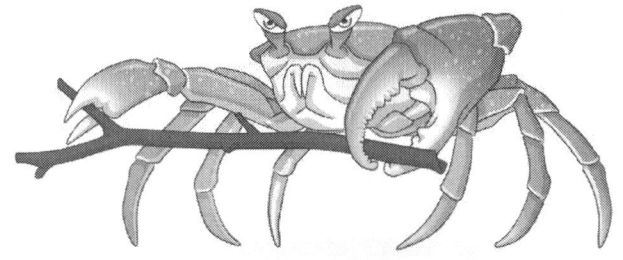

The Fortress of the Dredge

Meanwhile at the fortress of the Dredge, Princess Ariadne was now being held in a steel cage used for locking up rats. The cage had been moved out into the main courtyard so that the Dredge guard could keep an eye on her and not be concerned about her escaping.

With every tremor, the princess knew the end was near. She was slowly losing hope of a rescue from any of her fellow Atlanteans. The Dredge pretty much left her alone. They knew that Styx would be content to let her starve to death. That is, unless she would submit to becoming his queen, but that was never going to happen. Occasionally a rat or a pack of cockroaches would check out the cage and then move on.

Styx had been watching the princess from an upper balcony for some time. He finally turned around and walked back into his war room and yelled out, "Someone, give me a report. What are the Atlanteans doing?"

One of his lieutenants stepped forward and said, "The Atlanteans have repaired their outer walls and gate, but that appears to be all. Our spies have not detected any sentry forces leaving Atlantis."

Styx walked over to him and yelled, "So you're telling me that they couldn't care less about their princess?"

The lieutenant replied, "We have heard rumors that a small group did leave Atlantis a few days ago, but we have yet to find any actual sightings of them."

Styx shoved him to the ground and yelled, "You take whatever you need and find them, no matter what the cost. Do you understand me?"

The lieutenant stood back up and, without saying a word, left the room.

A short time later, the lieutenant and a detail of ten Dredge warriors accompanied by a pack of cockroaches left the fortress. Princess Ariadne knew that this wasn't just a patrol. It must be a hunting party looking for someone. Each of the warriors was carrying a lionfish poison spear. She knew they were probably looking for a rescue team from Atlantis trying to locate her. As they left the fortress, the princess dropped her head.

Suddenly out of nowhere, she heard a faint voice say, "You certainly are in a fix, my lady."

Princess Ariadne looked around and could not see anyone. She whispered back, "Who are you? Why did you call me a lady? Do you know me?"

The tiny voice replied, "You sure ask a lot of questions for a lady. I'm a lady, too, but I don't ask that many questions."

The princess was getting frustrated. She replied, "Where are you?"

The voice replied, "There you go with another question. I'm in plain sight. Just look down."

The princess looked down and saw the rust-colored dirt moving. She stepped backward, and then a small red shell came up out of the dirt. The small red-and-black-dotted creature flew up and landed on her shoulder. Before the princess could swat at the creature, it flapped its wings and said, "Don't hit me. I'm your friend."

The princess allowed the small creature to climb on her hand. It was an insect with a red shell and black dots on the shell. The princess said, "You're beautiful. What are you doing in this wicked land? Do you have a name?"

The tiny insect twitched her antennae and said, "There you go with the questions. If you promise to stop asking me questions, I'll tell you."

The princess nodded her approval. The insect went on to say, "My name is Tizzy. I'm a ladybug from the world above. When the earth shook some time ago, I fell through a hole in the ground with some humans. I found my way here, and because of my colors, no one seems to see me. I've been living off scraps I've found on the ground."

Princess Ariadne gave her a pat on the shell and said, "Well, my lady Tizzy, I am honored to meet you. I have never met a ladybug before."

Looking around at the surroundings, the princess went on to say, "I'm surprised you came to Undercroft instead of Atlantis."

Tizzy replied, "With everything shaking and falling all around me, I fled for my life and flew as far as I could and ended up here. No one seems to notice me here, so here I stayed."

The princess gave her a little hug and said, "This is no place for a lady. You need to come home with me back to Atlantis."

Tizzy flickered her wings and said, "I like that. When can we go?"

Princess Ariadne lowered her head again and replied, "That's the problem. I'm locked in this cage and being held a prisoner."

Tizzy flew around the cage and landed back in Princess Ariadne's hand and asked, "What can I do to help?"

The princess sadly replied, "Just keep me company until someone from Atlantis rescues us."

Tizzy replied, "I won't leave your side."

The princess smiled and went over to the corner of the cage and sat down with her new friend. Tizzy made herself cozy in the princess's lap.

Chapter 14
The Lost Empire

The Lost Empire

As the group made its way down to the cavern floor from Skull Mountain, it was becoming apparent that there were some strange objects on the floor of the cavern. The cavern was huge and went on for miles. The strange objects were also very large, and the Spinners could make no sense of them. To them, the objects almost looked like artifacts.

After a few minutes of walking, Pello dropped to his knees, placed both his hands on one of the jagged stones, and yelled out, "We have truly found the ancient city of Atlantis, the city of my forefathers!"

The Spinners had no idea what they had just stepped into. Within minutes, Pello and the Spinners climbed up onto one of the large stones to get a better look around. Now it all made sense. These objects were the remains of the lost city of Atlantis. Instead of large boulders and stones, they were really looking at collapsed buildings made out of granite and stones from all over the world.

As Pello looked around, he said, "If my fellow Atlanteans knew that the city of our ancestors still existed, this would be a sacred place."

Sam gave him a hug and said, "This is the Atlantis that the surface world has written about for thousands of years. There were some believers that the city existed, but most believe it is a myth."

Pello looked at the Spinners and added, "Now we must find Princess Ariadne and show her this place."

Michael replied, "I know this is important. But the real city of Atlantis is your home, and we have to find the princess and save it so that it doesn't suffer the same fate as the original city did."

Pello, still looking around in amazement, added, "Michael, you are wise for such a young man. We do need to push on."

Meanwhile Portagee had been looking around in the ruins below. He looked up at the others and said, "The Dredge have known about this lost city for years. There's clearly a trail leading off in that direction that has been worn deep into the rock floor of this cavern."

Keno jumped down next to Portagee and added, "I agree with my little buddy. I think we'll find the princess at the end of this trail."

Pello waved his hand for Michael, Sam, and Graham to follow him as he climbed down from the massive granite. Once back on the ground level, he said, "We must be very careful. The Dredge probably have this trail seeded with hidden traps just in case any unexpected Atlanteans ever came this way." He pulled out his sword and added, "Follow me, but keep a look out."

Even as Pello was speaking, creatures from the shadows were watching their every move. They were Blackie and two of his fellow rats. As the Spinners and Pello walked out of sight, Blackie said to one of the rats, "You go back to the fortress and tell Styx that a sentry and the strangers are on their way to him."

The other rat hissed back and then ran off through the ruins in another direction.

Meanwhile back at the fortress, Princess Ariadne looked down at Tizzy sleeping in her lap and said, "I wish I could fly out of this cage like you."

With her eyes closed, Tizzy whispered back, "You can."

The princess let out a soft giggle and replied, "Tizzy, that's what I like about you. You're a very funny ladybug."

With her eyes open, Tizzy now looked up at the princess and said, "No, really, look above you; those bars are almost rusted through. You can escape through the top of this cage."

The princess replied, "So what if I did? The Dredge would see me climbing down the bars or running across the courtyard."

Tizzy smiled and added, "I can carry much more than you would think. If you hold on to my legs, I can at least fly you out of the courtyard."

Princess Ariadne looked down at Tizzy and asked, "Are you sure?"

Tizzy began to flicker her wings until she was just above the princess's head. She looked down at the princess and said, "Grab my legs now, and I'll show you."

Full of doubt, the princess grabbed her legs, and in a few seconds, Tizzy lifted her off the ground a couple of feet. She hovered for a minute and then lowered the princess back to the ground.

The princess said, "That's great, but you can't get us out of here by only flying two feet high."

Tizzy twitched her two antennae back and forth and said, "We don't have to. The top of the cage is higher than the wall. If I can fly fast enough for a short period of time, maybe we can float over the wall as we descend."

Princess Ariadne smiled and replied, "I liked your plan until you got to the 'maybe' part."

Tizzy replied, "I'll wait for you on top of the cage." A second later she flew through the bars, sat on top of the cage, and waited.

Just as Princess Ariadne was about to climb the cage wall, she saw three Dredge soldiers walking across the courtyard in her direction. To her surprise, the Dredge walked by and paid very little attention to her.

Once they were out of sight, Princess Ariadne climbed up the bars to the roof of the cage, where she began pushing on the rusted section. With very little effort from the princess, the rusty bars broke loose from where they had been attached to the other bars. Minutes later she had made an opening large enough to fit her body through. Making it to the top of the cage, the princess looked at Tizzy and asked, "Now what?"

Tizzy began flapping her wings and quickly was flying above the princess's head. She looked down at the princess and said, "I'll build up some speed and fly as fast as I can toward the other side of the cage. Once I get to the end, you leap and grab my legs."

The princess looked at Tizzy like she was crazy and said, "Sure, and what happens if I miss your legs while I'm leaping through the air?"

Tizzy ignored the princess's question, flew about twenty feet away from the cage, and said, "Start running. Here I come." A second later Tizzy was flying as fast as she could toward the cage.

Before Princess Ariadne could move, Tizzy had passed her. Princess Ariadne yelled out, "Holy Zeus!" and started running across the bars to catch up to Tizzy. Just as Tizzy flew over the edge of the bars, Princess Ariadne leaped out into midair and just caught Tizzy's legs.

The sudden pull on Tizzy's legs caused her to drop two feet in an instant. The two were flying toward the fortress wall and slowing losing attitude. By the time they reached the wall, Princess Ariadne's feet touched the top of the wall. She began running across the wall while still holding on to Tizzy's legs.

Once to the edge, the princess leaped again, and they were now floating down to the ground on the outside of the fortress. The pair landed safely on the ground. The princess gave Tizzy a hug, and the two scurried off into the cover of the rocks surrounding the fortress.

Chapter 15
The Night of the Dredge

The Night of the Dredge

Hours later Styx walked out on his balcony to look out over the courtyard. He had just heard the report from the rats sent by Blackie. Almost instantly he screamed out, "Where is the princess?"

Seconds later the courtyard was filled with Dredge soldiers running around like ants. Styx leaped off the balcony and landed in the courtyard. Pushing and shoving the men out of his way, Styx made his way to the iron cage. Once he saw the bent bars in the roof of the cage, he yelled out, "Search the entire fortress! The princess has to be here somewhere."

Styx knew that the gate was locked and never dreamed that the princess could have flown over the high walls of the fortress. Seconds later, except for Styx, the courtyard was empty. All of Styx's goons were looking for the princess throughout the fortress. Styx paced around the courtyard and waited for his men to find the princess.

Finally, after several hours of searching and not finding her, Styx knew that the princess had somehow escaped the fortress. He walked over and began beating on a drum as hard as he could. He knew that his goons would return to the courtyard very quickly.

One by one, the goons, cockroaches, and rats made their way back to the courtyard, and all were empty handed.

Styx was surprised that neither the cockroaches nor the rats had even picked up a scent of the princess.

Just as he was about to speak, another tremor struck the fortress and knocked Styx off his feet. Even Styx was now, in the back of his mind, beginning to wonder why there had been all these tremors over such a short period of time.

Styx stood back up and yelled, "Get me the princess! I want everyone out on the search to find her before the Atlanteans' search party finds her. If any of you do cross paths with the search party, destroy it! Now go!"

Once again the courtyard cleared in seconds. With a detachment of his best guards and a pack of cockroaches and rats, Styx stomped out through the fortress gate. Once outside the fortress, Styx looked at the two rats and yelled, "Take me in the direction of Blackie. The princess might be heading in the same direction. If not, we'll put an end to the Atlanteans' search party."

The two rats obeyed his command and took off in that direction. The pack of cockroaches was close behind them.

While Princess Ariadne and Tizzy were trying to find their way out of the Dredge kingdom, Pello and the Spinners were still making their way through the lost city. Even though the city was mostly destroyed and had been lost through the ages, what was left was still massive, especially when you are only two inches tall.

After walking for a day in the lost city, the small search party decided to make camp for the night in an area just off the main trail through the city. They found what must have been an old side street, where they hoped to rest for a while without being noticed by the Dredge or their spies.

The Spinners had a difficult time adapting to the fact that there was no day or night in the underworld. With no darkness, it was harder for them to fall to sleep. At least in Undercroft, without the brilliance of the natural crystals, the Spinners had an easier time sleeping.

Not far from the lost city, the princess and Tizzy came across a dampish area that was a forest of mushrooms, mold, and mildew. This was a cavern where the Dredge harvested most of their food. Princess Ariadne looked down at Tizzy and said, "I'm not sure if I want to go into that awful-looking place."

After looking around, Tizzy replied, "We could go back, or if you want, I could fly around the outer edges to see if there is another way around this place."

Just then they both heard sounds of something or someone not far behind them.

Princess Ariadne reached down, picked up Tizzy, and said, "We don't have a choice. We're about to have visitors."

With Tizzy in her arms, they quickly disappeared into the mushroom forest. As they moved deeper into the forest, the princess said, "I'm so hungry that I think I could eat one of these huge mushrooms."

Just then they came across a dead cockroach. Tizzy looked down at it and said, "I think the cockroach was hungry, too. Maybe you should pass on that snack for a while."

The princess smiled and replied, "I trust your judgment, Tizzy. Let's continue on."

The pair continued on for several hours. Finally, they came across a small opening in the mushroom forest. The floor of the clearing was a soft, white color and appeared to be perfectly smooth. As the princess walked across it, she noticed that the surface was very soft and squishy.

Princess Ariadne looked over at Tizzy as she flew next to her and said, "This is the softest sand I have ever walked on."

A few seconds later, she sank to her knees. It was as if the soft surface of the floor were sucking her in. A second later as she struggled, the princess sank to her waist.

Tizzy began flying in circles and yelling out, "What to do? What to do?"

All of a sudden, Princess Ariadne heard a familiar voice say, "Princess, you're in a pool of quick mold. The more you struggle, the more you will sink."

The princess looked up to see a familiar figure hopping from mushroom to mushroom. It was Weezer! The princess yelled out as she continued to slowly sink, "Weezer, you and Tizzy need to leave this wretched place before it swallows you both up, too!"

Weezer would not stand for that. He began jumping up and down, over and over, on the edge of a giant mushroom. He looked at Tizzy and said, "Come over here and push as hard as you can." Tizzy immediately began flying into the mushroom, over and over again.

Princess Ariadne could now see that they were trying to knock down the mushroom into the mold pit. Weezer could see that the princess was about out of time. She was now up to her shoulders in the mold.

Weezer yelled out, "Hit harder!" As the princess's head was sinking out of sight, both Weezer and Tizzy hit the tilting mushroom again and caused it to crash into the mold just as the princess sank out of sight.

Weezer reached down through the mold with both front legs and tried to locate the princess. After five seconds, with tears in his eyes, he said, "I've failed Princess Ariadne. She's gone."

A second later Weezer and Tizzy heard a clawing noise on the other side of the mushroom. Looking over to the other side of the trunk of the mushroom, they saw two hands clawing into the mushroom. Tizzy yelled out, "It's the princess!" Both Tizzy and Weezer each grabbed one of her arms and helped to pull her up onto the mushroom.

Princess Ariadne coughed and choked for a few minutes. Finally she sat up and gave Weezer and Tizzy a big hug. She looked at Weezer and said, "Weezer, I don't know where you came from, but I'm sure glad you did."

If Weezer could blush, he would have. Weezer replied, "My princess, I just got lucky. I've been lost for days and couldn't find my way back to Atlantis."

Princess Ariadne gave him another hug and said, "Well, I'm sure glad you were lost and found me." She looked over at Tizzy and added, "You're the best, too. I wouldn't be here without you, either."

Weezer began jumping up and down. With a puzzled look on her face, Princess Ariadne asked, "What is it Weezer?"

Weezer leaped back onto the ground and said, "You'd better get moving, my princess; the mushroom is beginning to sink into the mold pit."

Princess Ariadne could see he was right. She jumped to her feet and scrambled off the mushroom. Tizzy flicked her wings and lifted off the mushroom. Seconds later the mushroom sank out of sight into the mold pit.

The princess brushed herself off and said, "Since we're all lost, we'll keep moving in the opposite direction of the Dredge fortress." Without saying another word, the trio continued its journey through the mushroom forest.

Back in the lost city, it had been several hours since the Spinners and Pello had stopped to rest. Just as Portagee was getting restless and waking up, he found a hand covering his mouth. His eyes were now wide. It was Pello's hand. He was trying to keep Portagee quiet.

Pello whispered into Portagee's ear, "Something is coming."

Pello let go of Portagee and pulled out his sword and slowly moved over to the edge of the wall they had been resting behind. He raised his sword above his head, ready to strike. He stepped out from behind the wall. In that split second, he was ready to swing his sword, but he stopped dead in his tracks. It was Michael. He had gone for a walk.

Just as Pello was about to lecture Michael, Portagee screamed out, "Look out, above!"

Pello turned around and swung his sword above his head. In an instant, he had impaled one of Styx's black rats. The rat fell on top of Pello and pinned him down. The Spinners rushed to his aid and pulled the dead rat off of Pello. Pello stood up, and as he pulled out the sword from the rat, he said, "This is not a good sign."

With a concerned look on her face, Sam asked, "Why would you say that?"

Pello poked his sword at the dead rat and added, "The rats usually only attack if they're told to. This means that Styx has given orders to kill any intruders to Undercroft."

Keno added, "I guess that means that we're the intruders."

Graham chimed in. "Great deduction, my friend."

Pello interrupted. "Enough talk; rats never travel by themselves. We better get moving before more show up."

He quickly looked down the main trail and said, "I think we'd better get off this trail and keep to the less traveled side paths." He waved his arm and said, "Follow me, my friends."

One after another, they followed Pello down another side path about fifty yards off the main trail.

Chapter 16
Point of No Return

Point of No Return

Styx and his elite guard of glorified thugs were not far behind the rats that had some time ago picked up the trail of Princess Ariadne. Because of her multiple escapes, Styx's patience was now worn thin. He was on the verge of just doing her in. With the crystal pendulum already destroyed and the princess disposed of, Atlantis would be doomed.

A short time later, to Styx's surprise, Blackie and his pack of rats and cockroaches met up with him. Blackie went up to Styx and sat back on his hind legs. In the impatient mood he was in, Styx yelled out, "Well, what is it, Blackie? The only news I want is good news."

Blackie twisted his whiskers with one of his paws and replied, "Sire, we have found the hunting party and the princess with some companions."

Styx smiled and demanded, "So are they together?"

Blackie got back down on all four legs and walked around Styx and said, "No, at this point they are unaware of each other's location. However, in a few hours, they will probably cross paths."

Styx kicked Blackie in the side, which sent Blackie rolling across the ground, and yelled, "Don't toy with me, creature. Can we intercept them before they meet?"

Blackie got back to his feet and growled at Styx. He did not like Styx's treatment of him, but he also knew that Styx was his master. He replied, "Yes, master. You will have to follow me, and we will have to move out at a fast pace to do so."

Styx flipped out his arm and yelled, "So be it! Move out before it's too late."

In an instant, Blackie and his pack were gone. The pack quickly spread out to search a wider area. Blackie wanted to make sure that none of the Atlanteans would pass them undetected. Meanwhile Styx and his thugs lifted up their poison spears and followed behind the pack from a distance.

Pello and the Spinners finally made their way beyond the outskirts of the lost city. As they were leaving the ruins behind, Sam said, "Boy, I'm glad to get out of there. That was one spooky place."

Michael smiled and replied, "The whole kingdom of Undercroft is spooky to me."

They went on for quite some time until they appeared to be entering a small valley. As they were entering the valley, Pello raised his right hand and signaled them to stop. As he looked around, he said, "I'm not sure about—"

Then he stopped. Off in the distance, he could see something moving toward them. As the objects neared, he yelled out, "It's Princess Ariadne!" Without saying another word, he went running in her direction.

Keno looked at the others and said, "I hate to rain on his parade, but we've got company." He pointed to the ridges on both sides of the valley. The other Spinners now saw what Keno was looking at. There were cockroaches and rats impatiently running around as if they were waiting for something. The wait was not long. Styx and his thugs appeared on one ridge.

Graham was first to see Styx and said, "This is not going to end well."

Michael could see that Pello was so consumed with seeing Princess Ariadne that he was oblivious to the immediate threat. He yelled out, "Everyone, run toward Pello! We have to warn him." One after another, without question, the Spinners ran after Pello.

Styx had been watching the activity below with a smile on his face. Finally he had the princess trapped, with no way of escape. He looked down at the rats and cockroaches and screamed out, "Kill them all except for the princess!"

On command, the cockroaches and rats on both ridges descended. Styx looked back at his thugs and yelled, "What are you waiting for? Go after them!"

By now Pello had made his way to the princess. He grabbed her and gave her a big hug. He quickly realized what he had done and dropped to one knee and said, "Forgive me, Princess. I was so excited to see you that I lost control."

With a concerned look on her face, the princess said, "You might want to get your excitement under control because Styx and his thugs have us trapped."

Pello stood up, looked around, and now saw the predicament they were in. Seconds later the Spinners and Slink joined them. Pello pulled out his sword and said, "Everyone, circle around the princess and protect her."

While the others were doing what Pello had commanded, Slink said, "Slink says, follow me." He quickly began digging in the sand beneath him.

The princess looked down at Slink and said, "Slink, this is no time to bury your head in the sand."

Slink ignored her and kept digging and digging. Seconds later he dropped out of sight, leaving an open hole behind him. The rats and the cockroaches were now only twenty yards away.

Portagee looked down and said, "I don't know where Slink just went, but I'm game to follow him." Without waiting for approval, he jumped through the hole and was out of sight. Weezer and Tizzy were quick to follow.

With only seconds remaining, the princess followed Tizzy through the hole. Pello yelled out, "Follow the princess!"

One after another, the Spinners jumped into the hole. Just as Pello was going to jump, a cockroach leaped at him and knocked Pello off his feet. With the cockroach trying to maul him, Pello thrust his sword through the cockroach. Before another one could get to him, he rolled over into the hole and was out of sight.

A minute later while the cockroaches and rats were swarming around the hole, Styx and his thugs showed up. Styx grabbed a spear from one of his thugs and threw it down the hole.

One of Styx's thugs looked down the hole and yelled, "What are we waiting for? Let's go after them."

While the thug was still bent over the hole, Styx kicked him from behind and into the hole. The thug screamed as he disappeared out of sight. Styx looked at the rest of his thugs and yelled, "You fools! Look at the cockroaches. They won't even go down into the sink hole. Not one Dredge has ever come back from a sink hole."

He kicked some sand into the hole and said, "Princess Ariadne is dead, and now Atlantis is dead."

Looking at Blackie, he added, "Take your rats and cockroaches and scour Undercroft to make sure that the princess doesn't turn up again."

He turned away and walked off.

Chapter 17
No Way Out

No Way Out

After what seemed to be an eternity of blackness everyone, one after another, hit the bottom of what appeared to be a bottomless pit. As they were all getting on their feet and checking for injuries, a sudden thud and then a scream came out of the black hole.

Pello looked at the others and said, "Stay here. I'll check it out." Climbing on the back of Keno, he looked up into the hole. A few seconds later, he jumped off of Keno's back and said, "A Dredge guard must have fallen into the hole and was impaled on his own spear. He and the spear are so jammed in the small tunnel that even if we tried, we could never get past him."

Graham chimed in. "That's not a problem. There's no way I was going back that way to face those cockroaches and rats."

Slink walked up to Graham and added, "Slink says, oh, I would like that. Slink likes to eat cockroaches."

Sam looked over at Princess Ariadne and said, "That's gross."

As they all looked around, they appeared to be in a very large cavern with a fairly low ceiling. The floor of the cavern was damp and had small water puddles everywhere.

Princess Ariadne looked at Pello and asked, "Why have we never heard of this place before?"

Pello, still looking around, replied, "My princess, I'm not sure, but we should get moving and find a way out of here."

As they walked along in the very dimly lit cavern, Weezer and Slink were enjoying themselves finding dead water bugs. Portagee was now getting worried about their surroundings but was not sure whether to tell the others.

Ten minutes later Keno saw a fish on the floor of the cavern. He bent over, picked it up, and said, "Look. We have dinner."

Portagee now knew that his fears were right. He ran up to the others and said, "I've got some very bad news."

Princess Ariadne replied, "What is it, Portagee?"

Portagee went on to say, "I know why nobody knows about this place."

Michael asked, "Why's that?"

Now in a much lower voice, Portagee said, "This is one place we don't want to be in very long. It's an underwater cave. The tide is out right now, but soon when the tide returns, this cave is going to fill up with water. That's why we've been finding the dead water bugs and fish. When the tide went out, they were trapped here."

Sam asked, "I wonder when the next tide will come in and if the water flow will be fast or gradual?"

Portagee replied, "I'm guessing the tide comes in slowly because all of the rock formations in here are pretty smooth and not jagged from a rough, heavy, ocean wave."

Princess Ariadne walked over to her friends and asked, "Do you three think you can help us find a way out of here?"

Tizzy started flickering around in the air in a very nervous way and said, "All I can do is fly around and watch for the water rising."

Princess Ariadne gave her a pat on the head and said, "That is very good. Now off with you. Keep a lookout for the rising tide."

Weezer jumped up into Princess Ariadne's arms and said, "Slink and I are always searching for water with our sense of smell. So now we'll do the reverse and go where the scent is weak."

Princess Ariadne sat Weezer back down on the cavern floor and said, "Now off with you both. Go find a way out of here for us." Sniffing the air, Slink and Weezer went off in similar directions.

Just as the group was about to follow Slink and Weezer, Graham felt something on his shoe. He looked down and saw water lightly splashing on his shoe. He looked back up at the others and said, "Well, I think we just got our answer about when the tide is coming back into the cave."

Now the sense of urgency to find a way out of the underwater cave was greater than ever. Sam ran up to Weezer and asked, "Weezer, I know most frogs can swim under water, but how about tree frogs?"

Weezer stopped and jumped into Sam's arms and replied, "Yes, pretty lady. I can hold my breath for a very long time and swim under water. Do you think we won't find a way out?"

Sam quickly replied, "No, no, not at all, just the opposite reason for asking. I thought maybe you could swim out and find a close-by underwater tunnel to lead us back to safety. Can you do that?"

Weezer looked over at Princess Ariadne for her blessing. The princess gave him a nod of approval. Weezer jumped out of Sam's arms and headed off in the direction from where the water was flowing. He was out of sight in a minute. Everyone continued to follow Slink.

An hour later the group found Slink sitting on top of a junk pile. Upon closer inspection, it was pretty amazing. It was made up of long-lost items from the surface world. There was a one-hundred-year-old coin, a spoon, a diamond ring, broken ocean glass, and much more. With all the items being very small, it was apparent that weak currents had deposited these items here.

Even so, the water was now knee deep, and there was still no sign of an escape tunnel. Slink was very distracted by all of the objects. Finally Michael said, "Slink, you're not a pack rat. So forget about these items, and let's find a way out of here before it's too late."

Slink dropped his head as if he were a child having his toys taken away from him. He replied, "Slink says, I will, but can I come back for these things later?"

Pello replied, "Absolutely. You find us a way out of here, and we'll come back and get you this stuff." Slink wagged his tail like a happy puppy, jumped back down into the water, and slithered off again to look for a tunnel.

Although everyone was trying to stay positive, the rising water was putting a damper on that. The water was now up to their waists. As they waded deeper into the cave, hope was slowly giving away.

Princess Ariadne could see that Tizzy was tiring out as she had no place to land. The princess called out, "Come rest on my back for a while."

Tizzy did so immediately. Once on the princess's back, she said, "Thank you, Princess. I'll try not to stay very long."

The princess replied, "Stay as long as you need to, my dear."

The water continued to rise. For the taller ones, the water was now up to their necks. The shorter ones like Portagee were already swimming. But the roof of the cave was still a long way away, and they would all be swimming soon.

Pello heard a noise from behind them. He turned around to look and saw it was Weezer. He yelled out, "Tell us you found a way out, my friend."

Weezer yelled out as he drew closer, "I wish I could tell you that." The excitement of the moment was quickly lost. After a short pause, Weezer said, "Instead I found something else."

Just then Weezer began to rise out of the water. Everyone was puzzled, and then as he continued to rise out of the water, it became apparent that he was on Snorkel the sea turtle's back.

As Snorkel's head lifted out of the water, he said, "Well, it's good to see you all again. It looks like you could use some help." Slink and Tizzy were quick to find their way onto Snorkel's shell.

As the others swam closer to Snorkel, Sam asked, "If you don't mind me asking, how you can get us out of here and are you taking us back to the surface?"

Snorkel smiled as turtles do and replied, "No, I cannot take you to the surface. The journey is too long, because we are miles below the surface and these caves here are so hard to navigate. You would run out of air long before we could get there."

While he spoke, the water was continuing to rise. Now all of the humans were treading water.

Michael interrupted. "If you don't mind, we are running out of time. How are we going to get out of here?"

Snorkel replied, "Not to worry, my friend." He lifted his shell higher out of the water and lowered his head. He went on to say, "Climb up on my head and crawl under my shell. An air pocket will form there when I submerge under the water. The air supply will last long enough to get you back to Undercroft."

As Princess Ariadne, Pello, and the Spinners climbed onto Snorkel's head, Princess Ariadne asked, "Is there any way that we can go anywhere else than Undercroft?"

Snorkel replied, "There is one other place that I've only been to once before, but I was never there long enough to see how safe it was."

Princess Ariadne looked at the others and said, "I fear the Dredge. I would prefer to go anywhere else than Undercroft."

The Spinners all knew that Pello would not leave the princess's side, no matter what. Sam looked at the rest of the Spinners and said, "It's a no-brainer; let's go with the princess."

While everyone was climbing under Snorkel's shell, Tizzy was still flying around overhead. Princess Ariadne yelled up to her, "Come on, Tizzy! We're almost out of time."

Tizzy kept flickering around as she replied, "I can't swim; I can't go under the water."

Princess Ariadne replied, "I promise you that if you come down here, I won't let anything happen to you." Tizzy flickered around for another minute and then dropped down into the princess's arms.

Tizzy asked the princess, "You promise?"

Princess Ariadne replied, "I promise," as Tizzy crawled up under Snorkel's shell and out of sight.

Weezer was sitting on Snorkel's head. Once he saw everyone was in place, he patted Snorkel on the back of the head and said, "Let's move out, big fella."

Snorkel replied, "Aye, captain." With a massive swoosh from his front flippers, he submerged and began making his way out of the almost-submerged cave.

Inside the shell, there was a sudden jolt from Snorkel's movement. As Snorkel moved through the cave, which was now totally submerged, water was splashing in and around the feet and legs of his passengers, but so far the air pocket was holding. After a few minutes of getting used to the darkness, they could now see outlines of each other.

Sam reached out and touched who she thought was Michael and said, "Michael, are you all right?"

A voice responded, "Yes, but I'm Keno."

Sam felt a tap on her shoulder and a voice said, "I'm fine, but I'm over here." Michael was standing on her other side.

Princess Ariadne knew that Tizzy was fine. Tizzy was clinging to her back out of fear. The rest of the group were all doing fine; they just hoped the air supply would last.

Meanwhile Snorkel was swimming as fast as he could in the tight confines of the cave. Weezer was using the suction grips on his feet to cling onto Snorkel's head. Weezer was enjoying the ride, but he hoped that his friends were still fine in Snorkel's shell.

After a short period of time, Snorkel made his way out of the cave. Now all Snorkel had to do was to remember where the other hidden cove he had once visited was.

Chapter 18
Mystery Cove

Mystery Cove

With time running out, Snorkel was beginning to worry that his friends' air supply might be depleted before he found the cove he was looking for. By now even Weezer was starting to think about taking on air. As Snorkel kept a sharp eye out for the entrance to the hidden cove, he kept trying to remember exactly where it was.

Finally where he thought the entrance might be came to him. He could only hope that he was right. Once he committed to this, there would be no other option. The air supply in his shell would be depleted.

Snorkel began swimming very fast, winding in and out of the underwater rock formations, and searching in the direction he believed the cove opening to be. From above, a ray of light shone down through the dark sea. Snorkel was convinced that he had found the opening to the cove.

With very little time left, Snorkel gave a thrust with his massive flippers and shot like a rocket through the cove opening. He made a huge splash on the surface of the water, and waves went out in all directions and crashed onto the shorelines. Snorkel and Weezer patiently waited for their passengers to emerge from Snorkel's shell, but all was quiet.

Concerned, Weezer was about to hop into Snorkel's shell to check on his friends. Then all of a sudden, Keno fell out onto Snorkel's neck. Keno stood up and said, "Sorry, guys. I'm so big that I got stuck and couldn't get out."

One after another, the others came out onto Snorkel's neck and head. As Snorkel slowly floated toward the closest shoreline, everyone stared in disbelief. Sam looked over at Princess Ariadne and asked, "Are you sure you want to land here?"

Starting to question her own decision, Princess Ariadne said, "No, but I'm not going back underwater for a very long time."

This cavern was not like any cavern the Spinners or the Atlanteans had seen. The cavern was dimly lit and covered with a greenish-colored moss. There also appeared to be paths cut not only on the floor but also on the walls and ceiling.

A few minutes later Snorkel made his way to the shore and allowed everyone off. As he turned, Pello waved and yelled out, "Thanks!"

Snorkel raised one of his flippers, waved good-bye, and sank below the water. Seconds later an upheaval struck, which caused a large portion of the roof to collapse into the cove. When the smoke cleared, there was now an island of rocks in the middle of the cove.

Graham looked at the others and said, "I sure hope Snorkel got out of here before the roof collapsed."

Portagee added, "I'm sure he did get out, but he won't be coming back into this cove again."

As Pello was getting the group organized, he went over to Princess Ariadne, who was standing next to Tizzy. Pello asked, "Princess, do you mind if we have Tizzy fly around the cavern and look for a way out of here?"

Princess Ariadne looked at Tizzy and said, "Tizzy, see if you can find any tunnels that may lead us out of here."

Tizzy leaped from the princess's arms and flew out over the cove and looked for an escape tunnel.

Meanwhile the Spinners were all congregated in an area and looking at the moss. Sam asked the other Spinners, "Does anyone have a take on this? How can this moss be growing down here?"

Portagee bent over and ran his hand through the plush, green moss. He looked up at the others and said, "The moss must be able to grow in this environment because of the dampness down here and this weird lighting." He looked over at the pathways in the moss and added, "This is confusing to me. These paths don't appear to be worn; they look freshly cut."

With a surprised look on his face, Michael said, "You mean trimmed like a lawn service?"

Graham added, "Well, let's be on the lookout for someone with a machete or a battery-powered hedge trimmer."

Sam snapped back, "I don't think that's funny."

As the small group slowly got organized, Pello said, "Since we have no idea which way to go and Tizzy has not returned yet, I say we go on this path. It appears to follow the cove shoreline, and maybe we will find an offshoot path to a tunnel."

No one had a better idea, so the Spinners and Princess Ariadne followed Pello, with Weezer and Slink bringing up the rear.

An hour later Pello halted the group and said, "It's time we take a long break. We've all had a very long day." There was not going to be an argument from anyone. Within minutes, everyone was sitting down.

While the group rested, Slink and Weezer went out to explore around, and Tizzy, not having found any obvious tunnels of escape, returned. A short time later, Slink and Weezer came running back through the moss, and Slink was yelling, "Slink says, giant worms, giant worms!"

As Keno tried to calm Slink down, he asked, "I thought you like to eat worms?"

Slink shook his head and said, "Slink says, not these worms."

Portagee stood up and looked off in the distance and observed something strange. He could see something moving through the deep moss, but at the same time, moss clippings were flying through the air. At first he thought it was something like a lawn mower throwing off grass clippings.

By now everyone was watching as the object moved closer to the group. Finally Portagee looked at Keno and said, "Let me up on your shoulders, and maybe I can see what's heading our way."

Keno agreed and quickly lifted Portagee up on his shoulders. Now with a clear vision, Portagee only took a minute to determine what it was. Portagee began screaming, "Keno, let me down!"

Keno set him down and asked, "So what is it, my little buddy?"

Portagee was jumping up and down, yelling, "Run! Run! That's not a worm. It's a giant millipede with long pincers cutting through the moss."

Portagee was right; it was a millipede. It was as long as the Spinners were tall, with thousands of legs propelling it along, but the scary part was the long, razor-sharp pincers clipping through the moss like it was grass.

Sam looked at the others and said, "I think it's time to move out." By now they could see millipedes cutting through the moss all around them.

Michael added, "They must have just awoken from sleeping and are out feeding now."

Graham asked, "Yeah, but what are they feeding on?"

It was becoming obvious that the millipedes were being attracted to the group. Just then one of millipedes lifted its long body straight up in the air and looked at the invaders and started snapping its pincers together.

Pello yelled out, "Right now we should believe that their intentions are to eat us. Follow me quickly."

No one questioned Pello; they all just ran after him. Pello looked up in the air at Tizzy and yelled out, "Keep an eye out for a safe way to run that avoids the millipedes."

Tizzy replied, "OK, now go down that path on your right."

So far they were avoiding the millipedes; however, Michael noticed that more and more of them appeared to be following the fleeing group.

Michael was bringing up the rear and said to Sam, "I hope we don't run into a dead end anywhere, or we're dinner for these killer worms."

As they ran, Tizzy kept directing Pello onto paths away from the millipedes. This went on for about twenty minutes. Finally Pello had to stop and give everyone a rest. They had put some distance between themselves and the millipedes; however, the millipedes were still following them.

Still trying to catch her breath, Princess Ariadne bent over and said, "I'm sure sorry that I've brought you all into this mess."

Sam walked over to her and gave her a big hug and said, "This is what we do. We seek out adventures; however, I will say that this one has been far more than we expected."

Sitting next to Pello, Portagee asked, "I know we only have a few more minutes to rest, but what now?"

Before Pello could reply, Tizzy flew over them and said, "Flee now! They're coming from all directions except that way. Quickly! Follow me."

As Tizzy flew off, everyone followed her. A few minutes later, they found themselves at the water's edge of the cove. Michael looked up at Tizzy and asked, "Which way now?"

Tizzy was now flying around in large circles in a very nervous state. All she could say was, "They're everywhere."

Pello looked at the others and said, "We have no choice; it's back into the water."

As he stepped into the water, Graham asked, "Do you think they can swim?"

As they all swam out into the cove, Pello replied, "I hope not." Not long after that, four millipedes made their way to the shoreline. As they looked out over the water, they tried to remain as silent as possible in the hopes that the millipedes would not see them.

Then their worst nightmare happened. Two of the millipedes crawled out on to the water and began walking on it, just like they were on dry land. Graham looked over at Portagee and asked, "How can they walk on water like that?"

Portagee replied, "Unfortunately, with those hundreds of legs, their weight is so dispersed that evidently they can walk on water."

Pello pulled out his sword and said, "Well, I guess this is it." By now there were at least ten millipedes heading for them.

Portagee grabbed his arm and said, "Not so fast. I have an idea." He turned to Michael and added, "Michael, climb up on Keno's shoulders and do a cannon ball into the water."

Michael and Keno both thought Portagee was crazy, but they went along with him. As soon as Michael was up on Keno's shoulders, he yelled out, "Geronimo!" and leaped back into the water, holding his knees up to his chest and forming a ball. Upon hitting the water, he created a huge splash, which sent waves at the millipedes.

The others quickly got the idea and began splashing water in the direction of the millipedes. One after another, the millipedes began sinking into the water. Although they seemed to be able to propel themselves under the water, their instincts sent them scrambling toward the shore.

Minutes later they were back on shore and moving inland like nothing had happened. By now the Spinners, the princess, and Pello were all hugging each other. Tizzy was still flying overhead while Slink and Weezer were swimming around like nothing had happened.

As they were about to swim back to the shore, Graham yelled out, "Look over there! It looks like a half-submerged tunnel entrance." Graham was right; it was a tunnel entrance.

A short time later, they all had made it to the tunnel entrance. Looking into the tunnel, Sam said, "After the last tunnel filled up with water, I'm not so sure I want to go through that again."

Portagee replied, "Sam, that's not a problem here. I promise. There's no tide here in this cove to make that happen."

Michael added, "That may be true, but who knows what we may find in there."

Looking into the cave, Keno said, "Yeah, I know, but I'm not going back to have those big worms chop me to pieces. I'll take my chances in there."

Pello looked at Princess Ariadne. She nodded her head in approval. Pello pulled out his sword and said, "Follow me."

He quickly disappeared into the tunnel. The princess followed. Tizzy was hanging on to her back, and Slink and Weezer were on either side of her. A little more reluctantly, the Spinners followed the princess.

Chapter 19
The Dark Tunnel

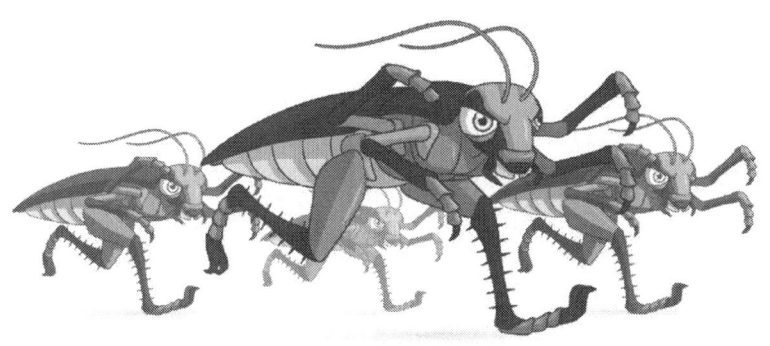

The Dark Tunnel

They were clearly in a tunnel and not a cave. As the small group continued into the half-submerged tunnel, the ribbed walls were quite strange. Since the walls were not smooth, it was apparent that there had never been water forcing itself through the tunnel, which was a relief to the small group.

The tunnel did have a surprising reflective glow to the walls, which kept it from being pitch black. Because of this, there seemed to be many shadows in the tunnel, which caused the group to think that they were seeing things that were really not there. Or so they hoped.

An hour into their journey, they had lost sight of the beginning of the tunnel that lay far behind them and still could not see an end to the tunnel in front of them. The tunnel so far had been very straight, with no offshoots or connecting tunnels.

As they waded through the water, Sam looked over at Portagee and asked, "What could have created this tunnel?"

Portagee scratched his head and replied, "The only thing that I can think of is that it's an ancient volcanic lava blowhole or steam blowhole. No matter what, it's been dormant for thousands of years."

Keno added, "I sure hope so. I don't want to get blown out of here."

As they kept walking, Portagee smiled and said, "Don't worry; you're too big to be blown out of this tunnel."

In the meantime, Weezer and Slink had moved out ahead of the group to scout for an opening. Tizzy had decided that the princess's back was the best place to stay instead of flying to who-knows-where.

Two hours later the group had caught up to Weezer and Slink, who were just sitting in the water and staring out at the tunnel. Pello walked up to them and said, "I see you two found the end of the tunnel, but why didn't you go through the netting covering it?"

Slink replied, "Slink says, I've never seen anything like this before. We thought we should wait for you."

Pello said, "Move back, and I'll cut through it."

Tizzy went into panic and started flying around in circles and yelling, "Don't do it! don't do it!"

Princess Ariadne looked up at Tizzy and asked, "Why not?"

Tizzy yelled out, "It's a spider web!"

Pello looked at the web again and asked, "So what if it's a spider web?"

Michael stepped forward and said, "Just touch your sword to the web and flick it."

With a confused look on his face, Pello walked up to the web and did just that. Seconds later a massive eight-legged spider came running out onto the web, looking for the cause of the vibration. The entire group stepped backward several feet while they all watched the spider look for something stuck on the web. Finding nothing, the spider quickly moved out of sight again.

Graham, who was already standing next to the princess, said, "That's a spider, and he's looking for his dinner."

Sam looked at the others and said, "Now what? It's either the claw-snapping worms or the bloodsucking spider."

Pello looked over at Portagee and said, "This time you wiggle your fingers on the web, and I'll do the rest."

Portagee snapped back, "Oh, yeah, let the little guy be the bait for the bloodsucking spider."

Keno put his hand on Portagee's shoulder and said, "Little buddy, step aside; I'll do it."

Portagee shoved Keno's hand off of his shoulder and replied, "The heck you will. I'll do it."

Portagee stepped up to the net and began wiggling his fingers in the web. No sooner had he started than the spider leaped back out onto the web. Portagee flinched and got his hand stuck in the web. Portagee yelled out, "Someone cut the web!"

Pello ignored Portagee's pleas for help, and just as the spider was about to strike Portagee's hand, he shoved the sword up into the belly of the spider. The spider fell to the cave floor and lay there silently. For the next few minutes, no one said a word as they all watched the still spider.

Meanwhile Sam helped Portagee free his hand from the webbing. Graham finally broke the silence. "Does anyone know if spiders play possum?"

Michael replied, "I think he's playing dead, but for real."

Princess Ariadne looked over at Pello and asked, "If you think it's safe, go ahead, Pello."

Being a man of few words, Pello drew his sword and slashed through the center of the web, causing it to collapse to both sides of the tunnel walls. One after another, the small group passed through the entryway into the new cave. As Slink walked by the dead spider, he sniffed it and pointed his tail straight up in the air.

The group all walked into the dimly lit cave. Portagee looked at the others and said, "On the surface, spiders tend to stay to themselves, but usually where there's one, there might be others in the more remote places in this cave."

Princess Ariadne replied, "Thank you, Portagee. We will proceed, but we will be very careful on this portion of our journey."

Sam asked, "Since you just said the word 'journey,' are we going somewhere, or are we just lost?"

Princess Ariadne walked over closer to the Spinners and replied, "You all do know that I am the keeper and protector of the crystal pendulum?"

She paused for a moment and waited for a reaction. As soon as the Spinners all nodded their heads, she continued, "I escaped the Dredge not to go back to Atlantis but to find a crystal suitable for becoming a new pendulum and putting our world back in order. Without that, Atlantis and your world that you know as Bermuda will be destroyed and swallowed up by the Sargasso Sea."

She took Sam's hand and added, "No, I do not know exactly where we are going; however, when we get to crossroads, I do sense which way to go." That was a good enough answer for Sam and the rest of the Spinners.

They now had time to look around and get their bearings. Michael looked over at Pello and said, "What is it with these worlds? Every new cave or cavern we enter is so different."

Graham replied before Pello could respond. "My guess is that during the Upheaval, as the island sank beneath the ocean, each of these caves became a miniature ecosystem unique to itself."

Portagee replied, "Thank you, professor." The others laughed although Graham was probably right.

This cave seemed more desolate than the other caves they had passed through on their journey. Maybe it was because of the spiders lurking in the dark shadows. The feeling was that most creatures might avoid entering this cave if they knew the threat in advance.

Pello and Princess Ariadne led, and the Spinners followed. Princess Ariadne looked down at Tizzy, Slink, and Weezer and said, "The three of you stay with us for now. No wandering out there in the darkness where the spiders are lurking."

Slink slithered around her legs and replied, "Slink says, not a problem, my princess. We will stay close to you and protect you."

Princess Ariadne replied with a smile, "Oh, thank you all for your dedication."

A short time later, Pello stopped the group and said, "We have all had a long day. Now is the time for rest." He looked over at Portagee and said, "You take the first watch and then pass it on to Michael."

Portagee replied, "Roger that, captain," and then saluted him. Pello gave him a strange look and went over to sit down and relax.

One after another, every member of the group fell asleep except for Portagee. He marched around the area with his sword in hand, leaning it against his shoulder like a little tin soldier. If the rest of the group hadn't been so tired, his movements probably would have kept them awake.

Actually Portagee was a little nervous. He did have a phobia of spiders. He hoped that his movements would keep them away from the group.

Instead it was doing the opposite. Spiders rely on vibrations when a prey is caught in the spider web. With all his moving around, Portagee was sending out vibrations throughout the cave that the spiders were picking up on.

A short time later, Portagee was getting a little tired. He decided to sit down on a large rock to take a short break. As he sat there, several web strands wrapped around his body. Before he could say anything, Portagee was jerked up into the air and out of sight in a second.

When his sword fell to the ground, Sam, jarred from her deep sleep, sat up quickly. She looked around and finally saw Portagee's sword on the ground. Just as Sam stood up to go over to investigate, she too was wrapped with webs and whisked into the air.

Several hours later, Pello ran around to the rest of the group and woke them up. Slightly groggy, Michel looked around and said, "Where're Portagee and Sam?"

Keno walked over and picked up Portagee's sword and said, "Portagee was having too much fun with this. My little buddy would never have left his sword."

Pello picked up some webs where Sam had been sleeping and added, "I think they were taken by spiders."

Princess Ariadne spoke up. "I hope the spiders are not bringing harm to them."

Graham replied, "If I remember correctly from school, the spiders may have wrapped them up in a ball of webbing to eat them later."

Princess Ariadne looked at Graham and said, "How horrible. We can't let that happen." She looked over at Pello and added, "Pello, we must go and save them at all costs."

Pello replied, "We will, but it's going to be hard. They appear to be on the ceiling of the cave."

Michael added, "I'm not so sure it's a good idea to split up in this cave."

Pello replied, "That won't be a problem. If you look at the ceiling of the cave closely, you will see that the spiders have left a trail of webs behind them. We'll follow the webs."

They all knew that there was not much time before Portagee and Sam became dinner for the spiders. One after another, the group followed Pello. Pello tracked the spider webs for hours until they finally came to a place where a huge patch of spider webbing covered a large portion of the cave ceiling. Pello looked up at the ceiling and said, "I'm guessing that they're up there."

Keno replied, "That's great. How are we going to get up there?"

Slink, Weezer, and Tizzy had not said a word since the spiders had captured Portagee and Sam. Finally Tizzy spoke up. "I'll fly up by the webbing and see if I can see them."

Slink replied, "Slink says, be careful, little one. I'm sure those spiders like ladybugs, too."

Tizzy nodded her head and said, "Not to worry. I'll be careful."

Tizzy flew up to the webbing and looked through the tiny openings in the web. Shortly after that, she flew back down to the ground and landed on Princess Ariadne's back. She spoke into the princess's ear. "I'm sure they're both up there. I heard Sam's voice coming from the web."

Princess Ariadne looked at the others and asked, "How can we get up there?"

Slink replied, "Slink says, Weezer and I can climb the wall and walk on the ceiling. Our feet are sticky."

Michael asked, "So how can that help get us up there?"

Weezer replied, "You just watch. I know what Slink is up to."

Seconds later the two scurried up the wall and quickly moved across the ceiling toward the large patch of webbing. Once there Slink rolled out his long tongue and lowered it straight down. Weezer ran down his tongue and said, "Michael, grab hold of Slink's tongue."

With a frown on his face Michael said, "Are you kidding me? His tongue is all sticky, and it's had bugs all over it."

Weezer said again, "Grab his tongue."

Michael grabbed it and said, "Now what?"

A second later Slink began swinging his tongue back and forth. With each swing, Michael got higher and higher. Finally Michael got close enough to the webbing that his free hand grabbed the web, and at the same moment, Slink snapped his tongue back into his mouth.

Michael was now able to grab the web with both hands and cling to the webbing. It took some work, but he finally inched his way up into the webbing. As he looked around, it reminded him of a very large tree house.

He somehow had to find Portagee and Sam before the spiders noticed him. Just as he was moving away from the opening, Michael heard a voice say, "Wait a minute."

He turned around to see Graham's arms sticking up through the web. Michael went back and pulled him up through the webbing. He then asked, "Is Keno coming, too?"

Graham snapped back, "Are you kidding me? As big as he is, the web would collapse under him."

Michael smiled and added, "I suppose you're right."

The two slowly made their way to what appeared to be the center of the web structure. At the center, there was a huge ball made of webbing that seemed to house something.

Graham poked his hands through the webbing in order to see into the massive ball. A few seconds later, he fell backward and began stuttering and pointing at the opening.

Michael quickly stepped over and looked through the small opening. After a minute, he looked back at Graham and said, "We'd better get Portagee and Sam out of there and fast." He went on to say, "That's a spider nursery in there."

Michael and Graham had seen hundreds of spider eggs in the ball. They both knew that once the baby spiders began to hatch, they would be hungry and quickly find the food cocoon balls with Portagee and Sam in them.

Without saying a word, Michael spread open the webbing wider so that he could crawl through it. Once Michael was in the ball, Graham quickly followed him.

It was obvious that Portagee and Sam were in the two large cocoon balls in the center of the large nursery ball. Once there both boys began ripping into the first ball they came to. Sam was in this one; she was totally wrapped up like a mummy. The top of her head from her nose up had been left unwrapped. It was evident that the spiders wanted their victims to be alive when their babies hatched.

Once Michael ripped off the webbing covering Sam's face, she said, "One of you, hurry up and get Portagee. I don't think we have much time left before the spiders hatch."

She was right; the tiny spider balls were beginning to show movement.

As Michael kept ripping off the webbing around Sam, he turned to Graham and said, "You'd better get Portagee while I free Sam."

Graham replied, "Roger that." He ran over to Portagee and ripped open the ball Portagee was in.

A few minutes later, Portagee and Sam were both free. As they made their way back to the tear in the web where they could drop back to the ground, Michael said, "Hurry! The baby spiders are chewing their way out of the web eggs."

Just as the group was almost at the opening, a large spider lowered itself down on a web line and blocked the opening. By now the tiny baby spiders were breaking out of their web eggs and were converging toward the tear.

Graham looked over at Portagee and asked, "Any ideas?"

Portagee smiled and said, "It's going to be quick fall. Try to land on your feet." Portagee pulled out a match from his pocket and struck it on the side of his pants. He looked at the other three and asked, "Are you guys ready? It's going to be a quick fall." The other three Spinners all nodded their heads and braced for the fall.

Portagee hesitated for a second, which caused Sam to yell out, "Come on, Portagee! Light the web."

Just as the baby spiders were converging on them, Portagee took the burning match and dropped it at his feet. In an instant, the webbing went up in a flash fire.

The spiders went scrambling toward the walls, while the four Spinners all dropped like rocks and mostly landed on their bottoms a second later. Keno, Pello, and Princess Ariadne ran over to help them back to their feet.

Keno looked around and said, "Boy, did those spiders leave the area in a heartbeat."

Michael replied, "And so should we. I don't want to be here if those bad boys return."

The group quickly moved out in the hopes of finding a way out of the spider world.

Chapter 20
The Crystal Cavern

The Crystal Cavern

A short while later, they came to what appeared to be a dead end in the spider cavern. As the group stood there, looking around and not sure what to do, Sam spoke up. "What now? Do we have to go back through the land of the creepy spiders?"

Pello looked over at the princess and asked, "Princess Ariadne, do you sense any direction we should be going in?"

Princess Ariadne smiled and said, as she pointed in front of her, "That is the direction we must go."

With puzzled looks on their faces, they all looked around. Graham said, "Princess, you do know that's a solid wall of rock in front of us?"

The princess smiled and replied, "Weezer, you and Slink please show the others the way."

Slink wagged his tail and said, "Slink says, yes, my princess." A second later Slink and Weezer ran across the cavern floor and began digging. Instead of a solid rock floor, it appeared to be lightweight sand.

Keno went over to look at it, bent down, picked up a handful of the sand, and asked, "What is this? It has no weight to it."

Princess Ariadne blushed as she said, "It's spider poop."

Keno quickly dropped the poop. Portagee laughed and said, "What's the problem, Keno? Every time you go to Horseshoe Bay and sit down in the sand, you're sitting in parrot-fish poop."

Keno snapped back, "What?"

Sam now chimed in. "That's right. The parrot fish eat the pink coral and poop it out, and it mixes in with the sand to make it pink."

Keno replied, "All right then. Let's all start digging."

Everyone including the princess began digging as fast as possible. Twenty minutes later they hit bottom, which caused a tunnel to appear.

Pello looked down the tunnel and said, "What's another dark tunnel to us? At least it's going in the right direction." He turned back to the others and said, "Follow me."

One after another, the group went single file down the narrow tunnel. Fortunately, the walk down this tunnel was uneventful. As they peered toward the end of the tunnel off in the distance, they could see a very bright light. The closer they got to the end of the tunnel, the brighter and brighter the light got, to the point that it seemed like daylight to the Spinners.

Michael looked at Sam and said, "Is it possible that we're back to the surface?"

Sam replied, "Oh, I hope not. There is no way I'm going home only two inches tall."

Portagee chimed in. "Don't worry, Sam. We're still miles below the surface of Bermuda. Whatever that light is at the end of the tunnel, it's not sunlight."

As the small group continued on, the Spinners all noticed that Princess Ariadne was now leading the way. Weezer, Tizzy, and Slink were all following close behind her.

Graham looked over at Keno and said, "I think that the princess knows exactly where we are going."

Keno smiled and replied, "I sure hope so."

Ten minutes later with Princess Ariadne leading the way, they left the tunnel and entered the new cavern. Everyone except for the princess was speechless. The princess spun around in circles with her hands high over her head and yelled, "Welcome to the world of the lost crystals!"

The princess was right; this was a cavern of crystals. The walls were crystals; the stalactites and stalagmites were also made out of crystals. Everywhere on the floor of the cavern were deposits of crystals.

Pello looked over at the princess and said, "My princess, how are you ever going to find the right crystal?"

The princess smiled and said as she walked away from him, "Do not worry, Pello. The crystal will find me."

As the princess walked off from the others, her three little friends were now closer to her than before. There was no way that they were going to let the princess out of their sight.

As the princess walked away, Sam asked Pello, "So now what? What are we supposed to do?"

Pello replied, "The princess will be fine. She now needs time to be alone. As for the rest of us—" He paused for a minute then continued, "Go ahead and explore and enjoy yourselves. We have nothing to fear in this cavern."

Pello looked over at a small clearing and said, "I'm going to go over there and take a nap."

Graham added, "I'm with him." He quickly followed Pello over to the clearing and lay down.

Portagee looked at Keno and said, "Let's go see what kind of riches we can find."

Sam laughed and said, "Portagee, don't forget that down here we're only two inches tall. Anything of value here won't be valuable on the surface. Or if it is of value, it will be too big for you to carry."

As Portagee and Keno walked off, Portagee said, "Yeah, yeah, I know."

Sam and Michael walked off in the other direction to explore the cavern. Meanwhile Princess Ariadne and her sidekicks were making their way through a large field of crystals. Slink looked up at the princess and asked, "Slink says, there're so many crystals to pick from. How will you do it?"

Princess Ariadne smiled and replied, "Watch this, my friends."

She spun around in circles; her arms were spread out, and her hair was floating in the air. After a minute, she stopped and looked around the field of crystals. The wait was not long. One after another, crystals began to glow in the colors of a rainbow.

Tizzy began to flitter around the cavern and, in a nervous tone, said, "Princess Ariadne, they're all so beautiful. Will all of these crystals work?

The princess replied, "No, the glowing crystals all want to be used, but the time is right for just one of them."

She turned and walked toward the glowing crystals and said, "Now watch this." As she walked, one of the glowing crystals went dim and quit glowing. The same thing happened again and again as the princess walked by hundreds of crystals.

Weezer looked at the others and said, "This is going to take forever."

Princess Ariadne wandered through the crystal field for hours. Finally there was only one crystal still glowing. As the princess walked closer and closer to it, instead of the glow dimming, the crystal glowed more brilliantly.

The princess bent down and picked up the crystal and said, "This is the one. This is the crystal that will save Atlantis."

She looked down at her three friends and added, "We have to protect this crystal and get it back to Atlantis. Time is running out."

No sooner had she finished speaking than another upheaval struck. Crystals all over the cavern were shattered to pieces. The upheaval caused the princess to drop the crystal. In an instant, Slink wrapped his body around the falling crystal and saved it from breaking.

Princess Ariadne bent down, patted Slink on the head, and said, "Thank you so much for saving the crystal. Are you all right?"

Slink wagged his tail and said, "Slink says, I'm fine. I think we should get this crystal back to Atlantis before something very bad happens."

Weezer laughed and said, "Slink, everything bad has already happened to us."

Princess Ariadne picked up Weezer and said, "Come on, Weezer; it's not so bad. If we all stick together, everything will be all right."

Princess Ariadne and her three friends headed back in the direction where they had left the others.

Meanwhile the others were all waiting for the princess to return. The sudden upheaval had caused Michael and Sam and the others to cut their exploring trip short.

As the princess walked up to the others, Keno went to her and said, "That crystal is too heavy for you to carry. Please let me take it."

The princess handed the crystal to Keno and said, "Thank you, but please be careful with it."

Portagee spoke up. "I'll strap it to his back, and I'll follow behind him." He looked over to Keno and added, "I've got your backside. Right, mate?"

Keno laughed and replied, "You sure do, little buddy."

Pello looked at the princess and said, "Princess Ariadne, it's time we make the long journey back to Atlantis."

The princess nodded her head and said, "Follow me." As she walked off, the others quickly followed her.

Chapter 21
The Journey Back to Atlantis

The Journey Back to Atlantis

A short time later, the princess found another passageway that led the small group out of the crystal cavern. They soon found themselves in a dimly lit rocky cavern.

As they walked along, Graham turned to Portagee and said, "For such a small world, it seems endless. Do you think we'll ever get back to Atlantis?"

Portagee replied, "I don't care when we get back. I just want to get back alive."

Sam looked over at Portagee and said, "Come on, Portagee. Let's have some positive thoughts."

While Sam was talking, they had failed to notice that something or someone was following them. A scouting party of cockroaches had stumbled upon them some time ago. In this terrain of dark-brown, jagged rocks, it was almost impossible to see the cockroaches. The lead cockroach had sent two of his fellow cockroaches back to Undercroft to inform Styx of their location.

Hours later the cockroaches made their way back to Undercroft. They quickly made their way into the fortress of the Dredge, where they found Blackie and Styx. One of the cockroaches began twitching his antennae back and forth.

Styx yelled out, "What is the cockroach telling us?"

Blackie ignored Styx's impatience and let the cockroach finish his message. Blackie looked up at Styx and said, "They have found Princess Ariadne."

Styx yelled again, "Did she have the crystal pendulum with her?"

The cockroach started twitching his antennae again while Blackie watched. A moment later Blackie turned back to Styx and said, "The cave was poorly lit, and they could not tell one way or another."

Styx yelled out again, "What use are these cockroaches to me? They can't tell me anything."

Blackie replied, "I think they can."

Styx was now on the verge of losing his temper. He yelled, "So tell me, before I squish these bugs with my boot!"

Blackie backed away a few steps from Styx and replied, "They can take us to the princess. If they have the crystal pendulum, we can destroy it and the princess. If she doesn't have it, then we simply destroy her."

Styx's facial expression went back to normal. He smiled and said, "Ah, yes, I agree. We will track down the princess and finally destroy her." He looked over at one of his henchmen and added, "Get me our best men. We'll move out within the hour and crush the princess and her little sidekicks."

He turned back to Blackie and said, "Get your rats and cockroaches ready. This time they won't escape the army of the Dredge."

A second later everyone in the room had vanished. Styx walked over to the window overlooking the courtyard and smiled as he watched his army forming below him. He knew that this would finally be an end to Atlantis, but what he didn't know was that it would also be an end of Undercroft if he succeeded.

An hour later Styx and his army stormed out of the fortress and made their way toward the unsuspecting Princess Ariadne and her followers.

Meanwhile Princess Ariadne and the Spinners had no idea that they were on a collision course with Styx and his army of the Dredge.

Slink and Weezer were way out in front of the others. They were supposed to be scouting; however, their hunger appeared to be taking the priority.

As Slink walked along, he said, "Slink says, I'm hungry. I sure wish we could find some bugs. Where're the cockroaches when you want them?"

Weezer was hungry, too, but he was not so excited about the cockroaches. He looked over at Slink and said, "You'd better be careful what you wish for, Slink. A pack of cockroaches just might eat us."

Slink replied, "Slink says, maybe you're right, my friend, but I'm very hungry." As he looked around the cavern, he added, "Slink says, I don't think there are any bugs in this cavern." Weezer nodded his head in agreement as they continued to scout out the cavern.

Meanwhile back with the group, Tizzy was flying around Princess Ariadne and keeping her company. The princess was relieved that she had found a crystal pendulum, but she was concerned about getting it back to Atlantis. She knew that Styx and his henchmen would still be looking for them.

Pello and Graham were bringing up the rear of the group. Pello wanted to make sure that no one was going to sneak up on their backside. As they walked along, Pello asked, "In the kingdom on the surface, are you giants there?"

Graham laughed and replied, "We are bigger than most, but there are animals there ten times bigger than us."

Pello looked surprised. He then asked, "How do you fend off such large creatures?"

Graham replied, "For thousands of years, we have hunted these creatures for food and sport and have almost made them extinct. Only in recent years have we tried to protect them and save them from extinction. Your world has done a far better job of preserving your environment and the creatures that live here than our world has."

Off in another conversation, Sam said to Michael, "I do miss home. Do you think we'll ever get back to the surface?"

Michael took Sam's hand and said, "I'm sure we will in due time."

Sam replied, "Yeah, but I hope we're not two inches tall."

Michael smiled and added, "Well, I know one thing for sure. If we don't get that crystal back to Atlantis, we won't have to worry about going home."

Sam snapped, "Don't talk like that, Michael."

As the group made its way through the cavern, it was apparent that the terrain was getting rougher. Pello knew that they were getting closer to Undercroft. He feared that Styx and his henchmen would be waiting for them. There was no way around Undercroft on their journey back to Atlantis. He knew that they would have to be very careful as they made their way through the Dredge Kingdom.

Chapter 22
The Valley of Darkness

The Valley of Darkness

With his band of rats and packs of cockroaches, Blackie was scouring every inch of Undercroft. He knew that Princess Ariadne and her friends would have to travel back through Undercroft to get to Atlantis. All he had to do was to discover the princess when she entered Undercroft.

Meanwhile Slink and Weezer found an entrance to another cavern. Slink stuck his tail straight up in the air and wiggled it back and forth to signal the others to come.

Pello was the first to arrive and he asked, "What is it?"

Slink dropped his tail and said, "Slink says, I think we found the way into Undercroft."

Pello replied, "Good, I think. However, we'll wait for the princess. She'll know for sure." He turned to look back to see how far back the princess was.

A few minutes later, the princess and the others caught up to Pello. She asked, "What is it?"

Pello looked down at Slink and said, "My good friend, go ahead and tell the princess the news."

Slink looked up to the princess and said, "Slink says, my princess, I think we've found Undercroft." Weezer began hopping up and down in agreement.

Princess Ariadne gave both Slink and Weezer a hug and said, "I'm so glad we have both of you here. Yes, this is the way into Undercroft. Now I have a really big challenge for both of you."

Weezer began jumping up and down with excitement and yelled out, "What is it, Princess? What is it?"

The princess smiled and replied, "I need you two to guide us safely through Undercroft and try to avoid the Dredge."

Slink replied, "Slink says, we're ready to go, Princess."

With that, he flipped out his long tongue and gave the princess a sticky lick on the cheek. A second later he and Weezer ran through the opening that led into the Dredge kingdom of Undercroft.

Seconds later Pello pulled out his sword and added, "The quicker we get moving, the quicker we get back to Atlantis." He pointed his sword toward the opening in the cavern and went through it. The rest of the group quickly followed in single file.

Once inside the cavern, Slink and Weezer were out of sight quickly as they scouted out the area for a safe way home, while Tizzy flew overhead and watched out for rats and cockroaches. The rest of the group followed Slink and Weezer.

Meanwhile the rats and the cockroaches had scattered throughout Undercroft in search of the princess and the crystal. Although Styx and his army of the Dredge stayed together as a single force, they were spread over a vast area in the hopes of trapping the princess and her band of misfits.

After hours of hunting, Styx was getting very impatient. He turned to one of his men and yelled, "Take a few of your men and go find that rat, Blackie. I grow tired of this search and want to put an end to the princess soon." His henchmen were gone in seconds at a full run.

A short time later, Slink and Weezer heard sounds out in front of them. Quickly they moved to cover behind some rocks on opposite sides of the path. Less than a minute later, two cockroaches came along the path with their antennae twitching; they were looking for the princess.

At exactly the same moment, both Slink and Weezer shot their tongues out like rockets at the cockroaches. The sticky tongues wrapped around the cockroaches and, like a rubber band, zapped them back to their mouths in an instant.

Slink and Weezer both smiled with delight. They were both hungry, and their dinner had come to them. Weezer looked over at Slink and said, "We'd better warn the others that this path is not safe to travel. We must find another way."

Slink replied, "Slink says, you go warn the others, and I'll wait for the rest of the pack and lead them off in another direction."

Weezer let out a chirp and pointed off to his right and said, "We'll head in that direction. You can catch up to us." He hopped off as fast as he could back toward the princess.

Not long after that, Slink heard more sounds coming his way. He was surprised to see two rats leading a pack of cockroaches. Slink knew that he was no match for two rats. He slapped his tail on the ground, making a loud noise, and hoped that the rats would hear him.

With the idea that the rats would follow him, Slink quickly slithered off in the opposite direction. His plan worked; after hearing the noise, the rats were now hot on Slink's trail. Slink would somehow have to lose them and circle back to catch up with his friends.

After Weezer had hopped for over twenty minutes, something swooped down at him. At first Weezer thought it was a giant bat, but he quickly heard a voice say, "Where's Slink?"

Weezer looked up and realized it was Tizzy. He replied, "Tizzy, you scared me."

Tizzy replied, "I'm sorry, but why are you by yourself?"

Weezer added, "Slink and I ran into a couple of cockroaches on this path. That means that there are more behind them."

Tizzy asked, "Did they run from you?"

Weezer smiled and said, "No, but they joined us for dinner."

Tizzy looked disgusted and said, "You both are terrible." She looked around again as she hovered over Weezer and asked, "So where's Slink?"

Weezer replied, "He stayed back for a while to lead the cockroaches off on a wild-goose chase in the opposite direction."

Tizzy replied, "Oh, dear me, I hope he'll be all right."

Weezer snapped, "He'll be OK. Now go warn the others to stay where they're at until I get there."

All in a fluster, Tizzy made a beeline back toward the princess and the others.

After a short flight, Tizzy landed on Princess Ariadne's shoulder. The princess could tell that Tizzy was upset. While she tried to calm Tizzy down, she asked, "What is it, Tizzy? What's the matter?"

Now much calmer, Tizzy replied, "Weezer said to stop and wait for him. There are cockroaches heading straight toward us."

By now Pello and the Spinners had also heard Tizzy. Pello walked over and asked, "So where do we go?"

Tizzy replied, "Weezer will be here soon and will show us which way to go. Slink is leading them off in another direction as I speak."

The princess looked worried. She said, "Slink is my friend. I hope that he escapes those beasts."

Sam joined the conversation. "He'll be fine. I know it."

A few minutes later, Weezer showed up. He pointed as he said, "We must move fast and head in that direction." One after another, the small group followed Weezer through the narrow rock opening.

Meanwhile Slink was running for his life. He had grossly underestimated the speed of the cockroaches and the rats. He had accomplished leading the pack away from his friends, but now how could he lose them and escape?

His little, short legs were getting tired. As he was running, Slink looked up and saw a stalactite hanging from the cavern ceiling. When he got close to it, he leaped as high as he could and just barely hung on to it.

As he started slipping down and losing his grip on the slick stalactite, Slink shot his sticky tongue up and secured himself to it. Next he quickly slipped around to the back of it and hoped that the pack would not see him.

Sure enough, they were all so busy chasing in the direction he had gone that they never looked up and saw Slink hanging there for his dear life. Once the pack of cockroaches and rats had passed him and were out of sight, Slink dropped back down to the floor of the cave.

Slink backtracked his way over the same path he had been on. He was sure that if the pack smelled his scent, it would think that the scent was from the first chase. Once he had put enough distance between him and the pack, Slink left the path and headed in the direction that he thought his friends were going.

On the other side of Undercroft, Styx and his army of the Dredge were moving slowly. Styx was getting more frustrated with each passing minute. He had only received one sighting in the last several hours, and it had never been confirmed.

How could Princess Ariadne and her small band keep eluding him? Finally out of desperation, Styx split his army up into four units to cover more ground. He was now letting his emotions overtake his wisdom.

Chapter 23
Time Is Running Out

Time Is Running Out

Hours later the princess and her band caught up to Weezer, who had been waiting for them for quite some time. No sooner had they sat down to rest than another major upheaval struck the underworld with such force that portions of the cavern's ceiling began to break away and shatter on the cavern's floor.

Between being knocked off their feet from the tremors and dodging the falling rocks from the ceiling, there was no place for them to hide from the impending disaster.

The princess and Pello knew that they were quickly running out of time. If the crystal pendulum was not restored soon, the entire underworld and the surface world would be destroyed.

When the dust from the upheaval had settled, Pello yelled out, "Is everyone OK?"

Sam yelled back, "Come quickly! I think Graham is hurt."

Michael arrived first and could see that Graham's arm was broken. While Michael was trying to keep Graham calm, Portagee was busy looking around for medical supplies.

A short time later, Portagee came back with several cedar sticks and sat down next to Graham. He looked at

Graham and said, "We're going to set your arm in a splint. It's going to hurt a little, but you'll be OK."

Graham looked up at Portagee and said, "You don't mind if I don't believe you?"

Portagee smiled and looked over at Keno and said, "Big man, hold our friend's arm still."

Keno nodded his head, and Portagee jerked his arm back in place. Graham let out a loud scream and then fainted. Portagee wasted no time and quickly set Graham's arm with the cedar splints and wrapped his belt around them. When he finished, Portagee said, "When Graham comes back around, he'll be as good as new."

Michael added, "Maybe, but not for a while."

Princess Ariadne had been distracted from the Spinners as she had wanted to make sure that her creature friends were all unhurt. After attending to her friends, she saw that Graham had his arm in Portagee's makeshift splint. She quickly made her way over to Graham and said, "I'm so sorry you were injured, Graham."

Graham replied, "I should be all right, but I won't be much good in a fight."

The princess smiled and said, "I can tell that Portagee did an admirable job setting your arm, but that won't be necessary." Graham and Portagee both looked at her with puzzled looks on their faces. The princess smiled again and said, "Now watch me closely."

She took out a small, oblong crystal from her pocket and began passing it up and down Graham's arm. As the crystal moved, it emitted a rainbow of colored rays over Graham's arm. She continued this process for well over a minute. Finally she stopped and said, "Portagee, remove the splint from Graham's arm."

Still with a puzzled look on his face, Portagee asked, "Are you sure?"

Princess Ariadne smiled and said, "I'm sure."

Portagee looked at Graham and said, "This is definitely going to hurt you more than it is going to hurt me." He paused for a minute and then removed the splints. After a brief moment, he released Graham's arm.

Graham began to gasp and then stopped. His arm was like nothing had happened. He looked over at the princess and asked, "What happened?"

Before the princess could reply, Pello said, "The princess is the only one in Atlantis who understands the full powers of the crystals. Many of us have been trained to use them for a few tasks, but only the princess can use them for healing."

The princess interrupted Pello. "We must go now. We are running out of time. The upheavals are getting stronger, and soon the caverns of our world will collapse under the pressure of the ocean above if we don't put the new crystal in place."

Not another word was said. The journey of the small group had just become more difficult because of all of the additional fallen rocks that now covered the cavern floor.

As they moved out, they failed to notice that their movements had not gone unnoticed. Blackie and his band of rats and cockroaches had been watching them since the last upheaval.

Blackie looked down at one of the cockroaches and said, "Take one of your packs back and find Styx and let him know that we have found Princess Ariadne and her band of traitors. Surely, with a pack of cockroaches, at least one of you will find your way back to the master. We will continue following them until Styx catches up to us. Now go!"

The small pack of six cockroaches was out of sight in seconds. Blackie looked at the remaining rats and cockroaches and said, "Spread out and don't lose the princess again."

Blackie knew that he would not survive the wrath of Styx if he lost the princess again.

Chapter 24
A Guide from Within

A Guide from Within

Princess Ariadne was now leading the way, with Pello following close behind. She seemed to know exactly where she was going and didn't waste any time in doing so. Slink, Weezer, and Tizzy were having no problem staying up with her; however, Pello and the Spinners were another story.

Sam looked over at Pello and said, "I get the distinct feeling that Princess Ariadne might leave us behind if we can't stay up with her."

Trying to save his breath, Pello nodded his head and said, "She's on a mission now, and there's no room for mistakes. She's now getting her stamina from the power in the crystal that we're taking back to Atlantis."

Huffing and puffing, Keno said, "I wish she would share just a little bit of that power."

Portagee chimed in. "Quit whining, you guys. Just keep up with the princess."

The small group had now moved into a part of the cavern with a very low ceiling. Tizzy had been flying very high and could see off into the distance; she was watching for the Dredge and their beasts. Now that she could only fly a few feet above the princess's head, there was no way to see more than twenty feet in front of her. This forced

Slink and Weezer to move out farther in front of the princess to watch out for the Dredge.

A short time later, Slink and Weezer spotted a pack of cockroaches heading on a direct course toward them. Weezer looked over at Slink and whispered, "What should we do? There's no place to hide."

Slink whispered back, "Slink says, you go back and warn the others. I'll handle the cockroaches."

Weezer replied, "OK, but there're too many of them to eat, my friend."

Slink replied, "Don't worry. I'll lead them off in another direction, just like I did before, while you and the others escape. Once I lose them, I'll circle back and find you."

As Weezer hopped off, he replied, "Be careful."

Slink moved toward the approaching cockroaches. Once he knew that they spotted him, he acted surprised and ran off in another direction. At first the cockroaches froze. They knew that skinks liked to feed on them. They quickly shook off that fear and ran after Slink.

Not long after that, Weezer found Princess Ariadne. He hopped up to her and said, "A pack of cockroaches was heading this way, and Slink led them off in another direction. The way should be clear now, but we need to move fast, before they return and pick up our tracks."

Princess Ariadne picked up Weezer and replied, "Oh, dear, I hope Slink will be all right." She then went on to say, "Thank you for the warning, and you are right; we will have to move quickly." She then asked Weezer, "Which way did Slink lead them?"

Weezer pointed with his stick finger and said, "That way, my princess."

To everyone's surprise, the princess replied, "Good. We will go in the same direction." The princess looked back at the others and added, "I know what you're all thinking, but don't worry. We know the direction from where the cockroaches came, and there will be more following them. By the time the cockroaches return, we will have passed over their trail."

Without waiting for debate, the princess headed off in the direction of the cockroaches.

Pello looked at the others and said, "You heard the princess. Let's go." Without question, the Spinners followed.

Meanwhile Slink was now trying to lose the cockroaches, but to no avail. To make matters worse, they were actually catching up to him. Finally Slink got the break he was looking for. He came upon a small saltwater stream. Slink knew that the cockroaches hated water, and because it was saltwater, they would hate it even more.

Slink quickly slithered into the stream and swam his way to the other side. Once out of the water, he quickly hid behind some rocks. Not long after, the cockroaches came to the stream and found the spot where Slink had entered the water.

Slink was right. There was no way the cockroaches were going into the water to follow him. Finally after several minutes, they moved on down the stream's shoreline in the hopes of finding a way to cross over the stream and continue their search for Slink. Not once did it dawn on the cockroaches that the princess was not with him.

Several hours later Weezer found the path that Slink had been on. Not long after that, the princess and the others caught up to him. Weezer asked the princess, "Slink was on this path. Should we keep following him?"

Princess Ariadne took a moment before replying and looked down the path for a while. It was almost like she was in a state of trance. Finally she turned back to the others and said, "No, we will keep going in the same direction."

Weezer asked, "So what about my friend Slink?"

The princess smiled and said, "Do not worry about Slink. He will catch up to us soon."
The group followed the princess.

Chapter 25
Which Way Out?

Which Way Out?

Hours later they found themselves nearing another cavern entrance. Tizzy had been flying around, keeping a sharp eye out for the Dredge. Suddenly she started flying around in circles. She was in such a tizzy that she couldn't speak. Everyone on the ground was getting very worried.

Tizzy finally flew down and landed on Princess Ariadne's shoulder. The princess looked at her and asked, "What is it, Tizzy? Why can't you talk?"

To her surprise, a voice behind her said, "Slink says, she can't talk because she's so happy to see me."

Tizzy finally said, "Yes, yes."

Sam ran over and hugged Slink and said, "We're all glad to see you." She quickly added, "Keep that happy tongue in your mouth." Slink just smiled and said nothing.

Princess Ariadne turned and walked over to what at first appeared to be another cavern entrance. She said nothing and just stood there looking into the cavern.

Pello walked up to her and asked, "My princess, is this not the way home?"

As she and the others walked into the cavern, the princess replied, "Yes, this is the way, but my senses aren't helping me now."

They were really not looking into a cavern. Instead it was an entrance leading into three tunnels. All of them led in a downward direction. They all looked the same, and the princess's senses could not tell her which tunnel to enter. All she could tell was that this was the right direction. In dismay, she said, "I don't know which tunnel to take."

Portagee spoke up first. "We either all go down one tunnel at a time until we figure out which one is right, or we split up in groups and try all three at the same time."

Pello replied, "We should all stay together and protect the princess and the crystal."

Before anyone else could say anything, another major upheaval struck. The cavern began shaking violently, and the ceiling started crumbling. There was no time to think or see what the others were doing. In the confusion of the moment and clouds of dust, members of the group escaped down all three tunnels. Shortly after that, the roof over the entrance to the tunnels collapsed, sealing the entrances to all three tunnels.

Meanwhile the cockroach pack that had been tracking Slink had reported back to Styx and the Dredge. At first Styx was upset that the cockroaches had lost the princess and the group.

After a pause, Styx calmly turned to his henchmen and said, "It is true that the princess and her band of misfits have eluded us once again, but the good news is that we now know where they are. They must be in possession of another crystal and on their way back to Atlantis."

Then out of nowhere, he erupted, swinging his sword in the air and yelling, "I want every Dredge, rat, and cockroach to converge on the last area where the princess was spotted. We have to find them and block their return to Atlantis. Stop them by any means and destroy the crystal."

With sword in hand, he stormed off in the direction where Slink had been spotted.

As the dust in the tunnels began to settle, coughing from breathing the bad air was all that could be heard. Finally a voice broke the silence and coughing. The voice said, "Can anyone hear me?" It was Sam.

Another voice answered, "I'm fine. Just a little stunned." It was Keno.

Pello spoke up next. "I'll be fine if Slink would stop licking my face."

As the three looked around, it was apparent that the others had escaped in one of the other tunnels, or at least they hoped that the others had done so.

After the members of the small group made it to their feet and had fairly clear vision, Sam said, "Well, we only have one direction to go in, since we can't go back into the tunnel. Let's hope that we run into the others and can get the crystal back to Atlantis." She then looked at Keno and said, "I assume that the crystal is still in one piece."

With a surprised look on his face, Keno replied, "Oh, no, I totally forgot about the crystal." He quickly took the backpack off his back and nervously opened it. With a relieved look on his face, he yelled, "It's still in one piece!"

Pello walked over to the others and said, "Slink, go on down the tunnel and see if you can find the others. We'll be right behind you."

As Slink slithered down the tunnel, he said, "Slink says, I'll find the princess." He was out of sight in seconds. The others quickly followed.

Meanwhile down one of the other tunnels, Graham, Michael, and Weezer were now assessing where they were. Weezer was hopping all around in a state of confusion and saying, "Oh, no! Oh, no! Oh, no!"

Michael went over to Weezer and convinced him to stop hopping. He then said, "Stay calm, Weezer, old buddy. We're going to find the others soon."

As Michael patted Weezer on the head, Weezer asked, "Are you sure?"

Graham joined the conversation. "Hop on my back, and we'll find our friends." Weezer hopped on his back, and the three headed down the tunnel to look for the others.

Not far away in the third tunnel, Princess Ariadne, Portagee, and Tizzy were already making their way down the tunnel. While Tizzy flew overhead, Portagee walked next to the princess. Portagee looked over at the princess and asked, "Do you still know the way back to Atlantis?"

In a disheartened tone, the princess replied, "Yes, I do. But we have to have the crystal, and I won't leave our friends behind, either."

Portagee smiled and said, "That won't be a problem; we'll find the others." They kept walking at a fast pace and hoped to run into Pello and the rest of the Spinners.

A short time later, the Dredge found the site of the collapsed tunnels. As Styx approached, Blackie ran up to him and said, "The scent of the princess stops at this tunnel collapse."

Styx signaled to his thugs and yelled, "You men and the rats, start digging. I want this tunnel opened quickly." His men started pulling out the rocks while the rats began digging. Styx could tell that he was closing in on Princess

Ariadne and the crystal. He could barely keep his emotions to himself.

No more than an hour after they had started digging, one of the rats broke through the rubble into one of the collapsed tunnels. Minutes later Blackie ran up Styx and said, "One of my rats has broken through into the tunnel. What is your command?"

Styx looked down at Blackie and said, "Let him track the princess while we get the passage opened up large enough for us to pass through." Blackie turned and ran back to the small passageway.

Finally Pello, Sam, Keno, and Slink made their way to the end of the tunnel, where it opened up into another cavern. With a frustrated look on her face, Sam asked Pello, "For such a tiny underworld, do these caves never end? Are we ever going to make it back to Atlantis?"

Pello put his arm around her and gave her a hug and said, "I know that this all seems hopeless, but there is light at the end of the tunnel."

Keno added, "Yeah, I know, but not at the end of this tunnel."

Sam wiped her eyes and said, "Thanks, Keno. I was just almost starting to feel better." Before Sam could say another word, Slink jumped up and gave her a big lick on the face.

Sam pointed her finger at Slink and said, "Would you stop doing that?" She paused for a second and added, "But thank you anyway."

Slink, wagging his tail, said, "Slink says, you're welcome."

Pello looked at Slink and said, "Go use that long tongue of yours for something constructive and see if you can pick up the scent of Princess Ariadne." After hearing the princess's name, Slink was gone in a second to find her.

Pello looked at the others and said, "We'd better get moving. Slink won't stop now until he finds Princess Ariadne." Pello followed Slink at a fast pace; Sam and Keno were close behind.

The tunnel Graham, Michael, and Weezer were in seemed to be heading in a downward direction. Michael and Graham were both worried that this was not a good sign, especially since it appeared to be getting warmer. Michael looked at Weezer, who was still on Graham's back, and asked, "Weezer, how are you getting along in this heat?"

Weezer replied, "I'm fine, but my skin is starting to dry out. We might need to find some water soon so that I can soak for a few minutes."

As they continued on into the tunnel, they finally came to an end, and their worst fears became a reality. They were staring at a cavern full of hot-steam ponds that must have been heated by some type of volcanic lava.

Graham looking over the cavern said, "There is no way that Weezer will make it through this cavern. In fact we may not, either." Looking over at Michael, he asked, "What are we going to do?"

Michael thought for a minute and replied, "There must be some air vents or passages out of here." He then pointed toward the cavern and added, "Look. The steam is not gathering anywhere. There is no fog in the cavern, so it must be escaping somewhere. All we have to do is find where."

No sooner had Michael quit talking than several of the ponds erupted into small geysers and spewed scalding, hot water everywhere. As the three took several steps back, Graham said, "Oh, great, now we're going to be boiled like a lobster."

The three waited for the geysers to stop spewing. Michael looked at Graham and said, "Are you ready?" Graham nodded his head. As Michael took the first step, he added, "You know that we have no idea when and where the next geyser will blow its top."

Graham replied, "Yeah, I already thought about that." He tapped Michael on the back to get him moving.

As Michael stepped out into the cavern, he asked, "Should we go fast or slow and cautious?"

Graham snapped back, "Run! As fast as we can."

The race was on. The two ran like deer through the cavern, dodged every pond they came across, and constantly watched where the steam clouds were flowing. With his suction-cup feet, Weezer was stuck to Graham's back for dear life and didn't move a muscle.

As they ran, geyser after geyser blew its top and threw scalding, hot water everywhere. The two Spinners were lucky and dodged the deadly water as they made their way through the geyser cavern.

Michael caught something out of the corner of his right eye. He slammed on his brakes immediately. The next thing he knew, Graham and Weezer flew over the top of him and sent all three of them rolling, one over the other, onto the cavern floor.

When they came to a stop, Graham looked up. He was inches away from a hot pool of water. Just then a geyser blew in the pool. Graham screamed out, "Geyser! Get out of here!"

All three jumped to their feet and started running for their lives. Michael yelled out, "Follow me! There's a tunnel over there." Without a second to lose, they scrambled into the tunnel and avoided the scalding, hot spew from the geyser.

As they collapsed on the tunnel floor, Graham asked, "What in the blue blazes did you stop dead in your tracks for?"

Michael, still panting, replied, "I saw a tunnel, and steam from the cavern was flowing into it. It must be a way out." Now that they were safe for a while, they agreed to rest and catch their breath.

Meanwhile Pello, Sam, and Keno were doing their best to try to keep up with Slink. Slink was on a mission to pick up a scent of the princess. Finally even Slink had to stop for a breather. When the others caught up to him, Sam went over and sat down by him and asked, "Any sign of Princess Ariadne?"

With his eyes half-shut, Slink said, "Slink says, no, but I'll keep trying."

Sam patted Slink on the top of his head and said, "We'll find her; don't worry."

Chapter 26
Cavern of Dreams

Cavern of Dreams

As Princess Ariadne, Portagee, and Tizzy made their way down the tunnel, they began to smell a very fragrant, sweet smell. The smell was like catnip to Tizzy. She quickly left the others without saying a word. The farther the princess and Portagee walked, the stronger the scent was.

A short time later, they entered the cavern. Off in the distance, they could see Tizzy flying almost uncontrollably all over the cavern. The contents of the cavern were unbelievable. The cavern floor was completely filled with every kind of lavender flower you could imagine.

The aroma was very calming. Both Princess Ariadne and Portagee walked into the cavern like they did not have a care in the world.

Once out in the middle of the field of flowers, Princess Ariadne looked at Portagee and said, "This is so calming. Don't you think we should sit down and wait for the others?"

In the same frame of mind, Portagee smiled and replied, "Yes, Princess, it would be nice to stop and enjoy our surroundings."

The two sat down in the middle of a patch of flowers and lavender green clover. Minutes later Tizzy landed in the princess's lap and fell asleep almost instantly. It was almost like the scent of the lavender flowers had put the trio into a trancelike state.

Sometime later, just by chance, the two tunnels that the other two groups were in merged into one tunnel. When the Spinners saw each other, they ran and hugged. Slink was very disappointed; he had thought he was going to see the princess.

Once the greetings were over, Pello said to the others, "By the looks of it, you found no sign of the princess and Portagee."

Graham replied, "All we found was a cavern full of hot, exploding geysers."

Sam added, "Well, at least you found a cavern. We have yet to see anything other than this awful tunnel."

Pello was now getting worried. He couldn't help but think that the princess was trapped in the tunnel collapse. He looked at the Spinners and said, "I fear that Princess Ariadne has been trapped back in the tunnel collapse. I must go back to find her. The rest of you must keep going."

The Spinners all looked at each other for a moment, and then instinctively Keno spoke up. "If you go back, we all go back. We're not splitting up again."

Sam added, "I honestly think that she and Portagee are ahead of us and not behind us. I think we should move forward."

Just as Pello was about to speak, he was interrupted by a voice off in the distance. It was Slink, running as fast as he could and trying to yell out something at the same time.

Unbeknown to the others, while they had been hugging, Slink had run off down the tunnel to look for the princess. As Slink neared the others, he yelled out, "Slink says, I found the trail of the princess! I picked up her scent."

Pello reached down and rubbed his head and said, "So much for going back." He looked down at Slink and said, "You and Weezer, take off and find Princess Ariadne, and we'll follow." Slink and Weezer were gone in a heartbeat, with the others following close behind.

Sure enough, not far away, the tunnel they were in merged with another tunnel, and this was where Slink had picked up the scent. As the group entered the other tunnel, Michael stopped and said, "What's that noise I hear?"

Pello raised his hand high into the air to signal the others to be silent. After a brief silence, he yelled out, "Run as fast as you can! It's a pack of cockroaches." No one needed to know anything else. They were all in a dead run almost instantly.

As they ran, Graham pointed out in front of them. He yelled out, "Look! There's a cavern a couple of hundred feet in front of us."

Michael replied, "I see it, too. Everyone run faster." They all knew that if the cockroaches had seen them, they could easily catch up to them.

Minutes later they came to the edge of the tunnel, where Weezer and Slink were waiting for them. Sam spoke up first. "What a beautiful place. How can something like this exist down here?"

Michael said frantically, "With the high moisture and artificial light, who knows? And to be honest, with the cockroaches hot on our heels, I don't care."

Pello looked over at Weezer and Slink and asked, "Why did you two stop here and not keep following the princess's scent?"

Weezer replied, "This heavy smell of the flowers has killed the princess's scent. We did not know where to go."

As the others thought about it, Graham looked behind him and yelled, "No time to debate. I see the cockroaches, and they see us. Run!"

The others took Graham's lead and ran after him. While they were running, Sam's foot got tangled up in a vine, which caused her to trip and fall. The others never noticed her fall and kept running.

Sam was slightly dazed from her fall, but as she was untangling her foot, she looked up and was surrounded by a pack of cockroaches. She hated little cockroaches and was terrified by these monsters. As she scooted away from them on her rear end, they kept getting closer.

Just as Sam thought that they were going to eat her, they began falling down one after another. Soon they all were on their backs, with their legs sticking straight in the air; it was like they were dead. Out of nowhere, something grabbed Sam's shoulder, and she let out a blood-curdling scream.

Quickly a voice behind her said, "It's me, Michael. Are you all right?"

Sam snapped back, "No! I was almost eaten by those nasty cockroaches." As Michael helped her up, she asked, "What happened to them anyway?"

Michael replied, "Graham thinks that this overwhelming lavender smell might be like a knockout gas. Who knows? Maybe it's fatal to the cockroaches. We know that they have a terrific sense of smell. No matter what, let's catch up to the others."

A short time later, they caught up with the others. Keno looked at Sam and Michael and said, "I'm sure glad you're safe."

Michael replied, "Yes, but for how long? I don't think the cockroaches will be able to follow us, at least for now. This scent is like bug spray to them."

Graham added, "Yeah, but I'm sure that the rats and the Dredge won't be far behind."

Pello interrupted them. "I think we've stood still long enough. This lavender field of flowers is not a field of dreams but a field of death. We don't know how long before it affects us. We must keep moving."

As they moved on, Slink and Weezer stayed with the group. Without their sense of smell, they could only rely on their eyesight, and being below most of the plants and flowers didn't help.

Two hours later Styx and his army of the Dredge entered the lavender cavern. After years of inhaling ash and smoke, they could not smell the lavender scent that the flowers were giving off. Blackie and his rats were another story. With their high sense of smell, they easily smelled the flowers.

While Styx was thinking what to do, one of the cockroaches flipped over on his backside. Styx looked down at the dead cockroach and asked, "What happened to him?"

Blackie walked over and sniffed the dead cockroach and said, "The scent in this cavern killed him."

Styx barked back, "It can't be much of a scent. I don't smell anything."

Blackie replied, "I assure you, my lord, it is real, and the cockroaches cannot cross this field of death."

Blackie's reply was not good news to Styx. He could not lose his trackers. He yelled back, "Then have the cockroaches run on the walls of the cavern and meet us on the other side. Split them into two packs going in each direction. Hopefully some of them will make it."

Blackie signaled to the cockroaches what to do, and they instantly obeyed. As they ran on the cavern walls, occasionally one would be consumed by the fumes and fall into the plants and flowers below.

Styx looked back at his army of the Dredge and yelled, "Move out! We have to find the cowardly Atlanteans and dispose of them." The Dredge spread out over the vast cavern of flowers and moved in the direction of the Spinners and Pello.

Meanwhile, not far away from the army of the Dredge, Pello and the Spinners were moving as fast as they could;

however, the sweet fumes from the flowers were beginning to take a toll on them. They were all becoming sluggish.

As they were walking along in a slight daze, Pello looked over to his right side and saw something red in color. He yelled out, "Stop! There's something over there."

Quickly he ran over to the spot. He yelled back to the others, "It's Princess Ariadne, Portagee, and Tizzy!" The red color he had spotted was Tizzy's wings.

By the time the Spinners made their way to Pello, he was on the ground with Princess Ariadne's head in his lap. With tears in her eyes, Sam asked, "Are the princess and Portagee gone?"

Keno ran over to Portagee and picked him up and started shaking him.

Graham yelled out, "What are you doing?"

Keno replied, "He's only asleep. Portagee's my friend; he wouldn't leave me." All of a sudden, Portagee started yawning and moving his head. Keno started hugging him and said, "I told you so. He wouldn't leave me."

After seeing what happened with Portagee, Pello started rubbing the princess's face. Sam quickly picked up Tizzy and lightly shook her. After a few minutes, the trio was back to normal.

The princess looked at the others and said, "Thank you for saving us. This place is dangerous; we must leave quickly." As she looked around, she asked, "Has anyone seen the Dredge?"

Pello replied, "My princess, we don't have a moment to lose. The Dredge are not far behind us and are closing in fast."

The princess turned and said, "Come quickly and follow me."

Chapter 27
The Trap

The Trap

Princess Ariadne saw an opening leading into another cavern, but there was only one problem. Packs of cockroaches were closing in on the entrance of the cavern from both sides. The princess looked at the others and yelled, "Hurry into the next cavern before it's too late!"

Slink, Weezer, and Tizzy were the first three through the cavern entrance. The princess and Keno were the next two through.

The cockroaches were already trying to block the entrance to the cavern. Pello drew his sword and was fighting them off as best as he could. He looked back at the others and yelled, "I can't hold them off much longer. Hurry!"

While he was running, Michael turned back to see if the Dredge were in sight. They were, and they were closing in fast. As Michael turned back around, his feet tangled, which caused him to trip, and he rolled head over heel. He struck his head on a rock and was out cold. By now Graham had made his way through the entrance.

Portagee and Sam both saw Michael stumble and fall. Pello never saw what happened to Michael. He was too busy fighting off the cockroaches. Sam looked over at Portagee and said, "We can't leave Michael."

At the same moment, they both turned back to run and help Michael. Upon reaching Michael, both Sam and Portagee tried to revive him. By the time they stood him up, it was too late; they were surrounded by rats and the Dredge.

Pello was now being overwhelmed by the cockroaches and had to break off the engagement. As he ran through the cavern's entrance, he could see the Spinners' predicament, but there was nothing he could do about it. All he could do now was run and catch up to the others.

When he did reach the others, Keno had a concerned look on his face and asked, "Where're the others?"

Pello shook his head and replied, "They did not make it. They were captured by the Dredge, and I couldn't stop it."

Graham looked at the others and said, "We have to go back and save them."

Pello replied, "I wish we could, but now more than ever, we have to get the crystal and the princess back to Atlantis. The Dredge will keep them as prisoners and try to trade them for the princess."

Keno added, "Yeah, but we all know that's never going to happen."

Princess Ariadne finally spoke up. "We will not abandon them. At the right time, we will free them."

Graham asked, "How is that going to happen?"

The princess smiled and replied, "Trust me. There will be a way at the right time."

Meanwhile Michael had recovered and found himself with Sam and Portagee; they were being surrounded by the Dredge. The Dredge thugs were just standing there with their poison lionfish spears pointing at the trio.

Sam could see that Michael's head had a pretty good cut on it. She said, "Don't let any of those goons touch that gash with those poison spears."

Michael replied, "That's not a problem, but I may stick one of them with his own spear."

Portagee added, "Now that's a thought, just not a good one. What are these goons waiting for?"

A voice from behind them said, "These warriors are waiting for me. I am Styx, lord of the Dredge, and you are lucky to be alive right now."

The three Spinners turned around and were shocked at the size of Styx. He was much larger than the rest and much more fearsome looking. As Styx looked his captives over, he said, "I can see that you are not from Atlantis. What world do you hail from?"

Michael spoke up. "You big oaf, we're from the surface world." Just then he felt something very sharp sticking in his back.

Styx looked down at Michael and said, "Little man, you move one muscle, and that poison spear will prick your skin. Then you'll be food for the crabs." Styx went on to say, "I've never met someone from the surface world. In fact, I didn't even know there were any survivors up there."

Michael stood there, motionless, not knowing what to do. Just as he was about to reply, Sam nudged him in the side. Michael knew what the nudge meant: don't tell Styx much about the surface world. Michael went on to say, "You're right; there're not many of us on the surface, and your world is a paradise compared to ours."

Styx looked slightly surprised and asked, "Why is that?"

Sam spoke up next. "The surface world is very hot and dry from all of the fires over the years. We have to spend most of our time inside to protect our skin."

Styx laughed and looked over at some of his thugs and said, "That's all we need, to have our skin dry out even more." His men laughed in unison.

Blackie had heard what Sam had said, and he knew that she was not telling the truth, but the bottom line was that he couldn't care less. He just looked at his fellow rats and walked away.

Styx looked at the Spinners and added, "We know that Princess Ariadne is trying to get back to Atlantis and is going to try to replace the crystal pendulum, but that's not going to happen." Just then a large upheaval struck and sent everyone to the cavern floor.

As the Spinners got back to their feet, Portagee said, "Mr. Styx, you know that without the crystal pendulum in place, the upheavals will destroy you too."

Styx laughed and replied, "Mind your own business. The city of Atlantis cannot survive without the crystal pendulum working, but the Dredge can."

The Spinners knew that Styx was wrong. Not only would the underworld beneath Bermuda be destroyed, but also Bermuda itself would be destroyed.

Styx looked over at his thugs and yelled, "Tie them up! We may need them for bait later." Styx then turned to Blackie and yelled, "Get those cockroaches tracking the princess. We have no time to lose."

Blackie signaled to the cockroaches, and they swarmed into the next cavern to pick up the trail once again.

Meanwhile after running for a very long distance, Pello and Weezer came up to another body of water. There was no shoreline around this water. The only way through this cavern would be to cross it.

The rest of the party caught up to Pello and Weezer. Pello looked at the princess and said, "Princess, we may be trapped here on the shoreline. There is no way around this water."

The princess smiled and said, "Keno, bring me that crystal."

Keno came forward and pulled the crystal out of the backpack. He then asked, "What now, Princess?"

Although it was very heavy, the princess took the crystal and lifted it over her head and pointed it toward the water. Almost instantly the water began bubbling. This went on for several minutes, and then it abruptly stopped. Graham looked over at Keno and said, "Well, whatever was supposed to happen, I think it failed."

Seconds later a school of rockfish came to the surface. The princess walked out into the water and gave the lead rockfish a hug.

As he ran into the water after the princess, Keno yelled, "Princess, be careful; that rockfish might eat you."

The princess smiled as the rockfish moved away from her and swam toward Keno. Stopping a few feet short of Keno, the rockfish said, "My name is Rocky, and who are you, my friend?"

Keno was now joined by Graham, and they were both speechless. The princess waded through the water back to the Spinners and said, "What's the matter with the two of you? Have you never seen a rockfish before?"

Graham was first to break the silence, "Princess, I have never seen a rockfish larger than me, much less one that can talk."

Rocky replied, "Don't worry, mates. I don't eat humans, not even tiny ones." Rocky flapped his tail in the water and added, "Princess, I almost forgot. Why did you signal for me?"

Now, with Pello standing by her side, the princess said, "We're in a bit of a hurry and need to cross this water before the Dredge catch up to us. Can you get us to the other side of this body of water?"

Rocky replied, "You and your friends climb on our backs, and we'll get you to the other side of the cavern."

Pello waved at the others and said, "Pick a rockfish and climb aboard."

Tizzy seemed a little nervous as she fluttered around over the water. The princess looked at her and asked, "What is it, Tizzy? You seem troubled."

Tizzy flew down and landed on the princess's back and said, "I am. Fish like to eat insects."

The princess replied, "You're probably right, but I promise you that you are safe with Rocky and his school of friends."

Tizzy's fluttering calmed as she said, "That's fine; however, all the same, I'll fly across the water."

Princess Ariadne lifted Tizzy up in the air and gave her a send-off. The princess added, "We'll see you on the other side, my dear." Because the waters were slightly rough from all the upheavals, Tizzy flew as high as she could.

One after another, the Spinners climbed on the backs of the rockfish. The princess climbed on the back of Rocky. Pello and Weezer were on the rockfish right behind Rocky. Rocky wasted no time. Once everyone was comfortable, the school of rockfish swam out into the massive lake.

A short time later, packs of cockroaches made their way to the shores of the lake, followed up by the Dredge and the rats. As Styx and the Dredge looked out over the lake, Styx looked down at Blackie and asked, "The princess is nowhere in sight. Do you think she backtracked into the other cavern or somehow escaped out onto the lake?"

Blackie sat up on his hind legs and sniffed high into the air with his long nose. After walking over to the shoreline, he looked back at Styx and said, "I smell a strong scent of fish. I think the princess got help from the rockfish in the lake."

Styx laughed and yelled, "Good. We've got them where we want them."

He walked over to the lake and dunked his head into the water and screamed something out. The sound beneath the water was muffled. Whatever he yelled out was only heard beneath the water. Styx stood up and backed away from the lake and waited.

He did not have to wait long. Soon the water began bubbling like a boiling pot of water. Seconds later a monstrous crab exploded to the surface and climbed up on the shoreline.

From the deep purple color of the shell, there was no mistaking who it was. It was Claws, the most fearsome creature of the Undercroft seas. The giant ghost crab moved sideways toward Styx. Once within a few feet of Styx, Claws sat down and scratched his huge claw in the dirt at Styx's feet.

Styx looked up at the mighty crab and raised his lionfish spear high in the air and yelled, "I need you and your army of crabs to take us across this vast lake and find and destroy Princess Ariadne."

Claws raised both of his front claws in the air and started clicking them. Soon the noise caused a band of crabs to surface from under the water. They quickly swam to the shoreline and extended their claws so that the Dredge could use them as boarding planks.

Styx looked at Blackie and said, "Take some of your fellow rats and cockroaches and load up on two of the crabs. The rest can stay behind."

He turned to his Dredge army and yelled, "Those of you who can go with the crabs, do so. The rest of you, go back to Undercroft and wait for my return."

As Styx made his way to climb on the back of Claws, it dawned on him that he had forgotten something. He turned back and waved as he spoke. "Bring the prisoners to me. They can ride with me."

Styx climbed on the back of Claws, and when the Spinners were loaded, he signaled Claws to move out.

Chapter 28
The Voyage

The Voyage

Portagee, Sam, and Michael were tied to each other, but other than that, Styx and the Dredge guards were paying very little attention to them.

Sam nudged Michael and asked, "What are we going to do if we get washed away by a big wave or if this monster takes a sudden dive below the water?"

Michael replied, "It's simple. We're going to get wet, and we'd better hold our breath for a very long time."

With a disapproving look, Sam replied, "You're so comforting."

Portagee interrupted them by tapping them both on their shoulders. He whispered, "I found some broken crab shells back on the shoreline. They're pretty sharp. I think we can cut through the ropes."

Sam smiled and replied, "That's a good idea, but right now we're not going to escape anywhere."

Although the crabs were not fast swimmers, they were actually catching up with the rockfish. Because the rockfish had slippery bodies, they had to swim very slowly in order not to lose their passengers.

Tizzy had been flying all over the lake and watching out for the Dredge. Unfortunately she found what she was looking for. After a few minutes of frantic flying, she caught up to Princess Ariadne and Rocky. Landing on Rocky's back, she went directly to the princess and said frantically, "They are not far behind us, riding on the shells of giant crabs."

Princess Ariadne quickly turned to look behind, but the high waves prevented her from seeing the clan of crabs. She quickly turned back and said, "Rocky, you and the other rockfish need to swim faster, or the crabs will catch us. Don't worry; we'll hang on."

Rocky splashed his tail fin in the water, signaling to the rest of the rockfish in the school. They quickly moved out at a much faster rate and caused their riders to hang on for dear life.

Just as everyone were feeling safer, a school of lionfish surfaced and set up what appeared to be an impregnable spiked wall.

Rocky turned his head back to the princess and said, "If we go under, you will surely slip off our backs. If we try to go around, they will cut us off."

The princess leaned up toward Rocky's head and whispered something. She then yelled out, "Hold on, everyone!"

Weezer and Slink clamped their suction toes to the side of the rockfish, while the others gripped as tightly as they could. The rockfish accelerated their speed, and as they grew closer, the lionfish puffed up, leaned forward, and pointed their poisonous spikes directly at the rockfish.

The rockfish were now at a point of no return. All the passengers gripped as tightly as they could; they knew that they were about to take a dive under water. At the last second, Rocky launched himself out of the water and completely leaped over the wall of lionfish and their deadly spikes.

One after another, the rest of the school of rockfish did the same thing, barely missing the death stings of the lionfish. The lionfish were not fast swimmers and had no chance of catching up to the rockfish. Without the element of surprise or a direct confrontation with their prey, the aggressive lionfish would fail. The passengers aboard the rockfish could now relax, at least for now.

A short time later, Claws and his clan of crabs came upon the wall of lionfish. Although the lionfish were no friends of the crabs or the Dredge, they made way and allowed them to pass. It was a very uneasy moment for both sides as they passed each other like ships in the night.

As they passed, Michael asked, "What's going on? Are these guys friends or foes?"

Portagee replied, "I'm guessing that since the Dredge use the lionfish spikes as spears, it's not a good thing for the lionfish. Removing them would kill the lionfish. Right now the spikes of the lionfish probably can't pierce the hard armor shell of the crabs, and the crabs can't do much to the lionfish. So it's a standoff."

With a frown on her face, Sam added, "Thanks for that in-depth explanation. So right now nobody except us has a thing to worry about."

Portagee replied, "You got that right." The three Spinners had nothing else to say. They knew that they were trapped until they could step on dry land.

The band of crabs with its passengers were quick to pass by the lionfish. There was no attempt by the lionfish to follow the crabs. The lionfish simply submerged themselves and were out of sight in seconds.

As the crabs hit clear sailing again, Styx looked out over the open water and said, "Blast it! The princess and her band of cowards are out of sight." He looked down at Claws and yelled out, "Can't you go any faster?" Claws ignored him and kept swimming at the same rate of speed.

Later that day Rocky and the school of rockfish finally made it close to shore. Because the water was shallow, the small group was going to have to wade ashore. Before heading to shore, Princess Ariadne moved over to Rocky and gave him a big hug. She added, "Thank you so much for the ride across the lake. We would have never made it without you and your friends."

Rocky replied, "You're welcome, but we must leave quickly and get to deeper waters before we get trapped in these shallow waters." Rocky slapped his tail fin in the water and shot out across the water. The rest of the school quickly followed.

Princess Ariadne, Pello, and the others waded ashore. Once back on dry land, Graham looked around and asked, "Are we any closer to Atlantis? Do we even know where we are?"

The princess smiled as she walked closer to Graham and placed a comforting hand on his shoulder. In a low tone, she said, "I know we are next to a lake somewhere in the underworld, but most importantly we are getting closer to Atlantis. Time is running out before the entire underworld collapses from the upheavals. We must move on and stay ahead of the Dredge."

Keno asked, "So what about our friends? The Dredge have them as prisoners."

Princess Ariadne replied, "Do not worry about your friends. They are still prisoners of the Dredge, and just like the Dredge, they are not far behind us. Somehow we will be reunited with them."

Graham added, "Yeah, I hope so, but not as fellow prisoners."

Pello interrupted, "Enough of the doom and gloom. We've got to get moving." He looked over at Tizzy, Slink, and Weezer and added, "Come on, my little friends. We need you to check out that cavern over there."

Slink replied, "Slink says, we will lead the way." Slink and Weezer ran off toward the opening to the next cavern while Tizzy took to the air and followed them.

Chapter 29
The Forgotten Land

The Forgotten Land

Princess Ariadne, followed by Pello, Keno, and Graham, entered the adjoining cavern. Although the cavern was a surprise to everyone, Princess Ariadne remembered stories from her parents about this cavern.

As they walked along, Princess Ariadne said, "This is the Forgotten Land. I remember that when I was a very little girl, my parents told me about it."

She went on to say, "More than a thousand years ago, the Atlanteans felt that it was time to expand their kingdom into a new area of the underworld. After looking for years, they finally found a fertile cavern where they could grow just about any crop that was available to Atlantis.

"A large group of Atlanteans volunteered to move to the new land and establish a colony. For a number of years, all went well, except for the occasional attack from the Dredge. Just as the colony was becoming self-sufficient, the Dredge discovered that the cavern roof had leaking cracks in it and was just beneath a saltwater lake.

"By dropping a boulder from above into the water, the Dredge made the entire lake break through the roof of the colony and wipe out the entire population of the colony. The saltwater stagnated, thus ruining the fertile land and making it impossible for the colonists to ever grow crops again."

Graham added, "That was terrible. Did the people from Atlantis ever try to build a new colony again?"

The princess replied, "No, Atlantis felt they could never protect an outlying colony from the Dredge. So we have improved our farming skills within our own borders to feed our population."

As they walked through the Forgotten Land, it was apparent that the foul smell of the saltwater was everywhere. There were some old stone shacks in ruins, and nothing anywhere was alive. Not even bugs. The princess had nothing more to say. She kept walking without looking anywhere except where she was going.

A short time later, Styx and the Dredge made landfall. As his goons were unloading from the backs of the crabs, he walked over to Claws and said, "Claws, take a small group of my men and wait for us at Atlantis, just in case the princess gets there before we can stop her."

Claws pounded one of his massive claws on the shoreline, smashing the rocks and causing them to fall into the lake.

Sam looked at the other Spinners and said, "Oh, great, I hope we don't have to go with him. He's got a very bad temper."

Hearing Sam, Styx yelled out, "Little lady, you'd better keep quiet, or I will make you go with Claws."

That was all Sam needed to hear. She smiled and kept her mouth closed.

With his fellow crabs and half of the remaining army, Claws left to head directly by water to Atlantis. Styx was very confident that he could catch and destroy the princess and the crystal even with a small regiment of Dredge goons. Even if they evaded capture, the Dredge waiting for them at the gates of Atlantis would destroy them.

As the Dredge marched into the next cavern, Michael whispered to the other Spinners, "The mighty Dredge army keeps getting divided up into smaller groups. I think that now whenever the opportunity presents itself, we should try to disappear." The other two nodded in agreement as they walked along.

The Dredge had a very different view of the Forgotten Land. To them, it was almost a shrine that represented one of the few times they had decisively beaten the Atlanteans over the years.

Styx knew that he was running out of time. No matter what he did, he wasn't closing the gap on the princess. So far he hadn't even been able to use his prisoners to gain any leverage. As Styx and his goons moved across the desolate wasteland, it finally came to him how to defeat the princess and her tiny band.

Styx stopped and yelled out, "Bring me the rats!"

Minutes later Blackie and his rats made their way back to Styx. Blackie walked up to Styx on all fours and then sat back on his hind legs and said, "Master, what is it that you want?"

Styx walked over to Blackie and said, "Until now, I have had you and the cockroaches track and follow those cowards. That stops now!"

Blackie rose up off his two hind legs and asked, "And then what, master?"

Styx raised his poison spear high in the air and yelled, "They can't outrun you and your pack of cockroaches. Catch up to them and separate them and finish them off, but do not under any circumstances harm the princess. I will take care of her when we catch up to you. Get your fellow rats and cockroaches and attack now!"

Blackie turned and growled at the other rats and the cockroaches and ran like wildfire through the Dredge goons. The other rats and cockroaches were quick to follow him.

During all the commotion, Michael looked at Sam and Portagee and said, "I think our window of opportunity has just presented us with a means to escape."

The Spinners quickly pulled out their fragments of crab shells and began cutting at their bindings. In no time, Michael and Portagee were free, and then Michael turned to help a struggling Sam cut through her bindings.

Portagee yelled to the others, "Follow me! There's a pile of rocks over there to hide behind." One after another, they ran and hid among the large rocks.

During all of the excitement, Styx and his goons had failed to notice that the Spinners had escaped. With his spear still high over his head, Styx yelled out, "Follow the rats."

In a high frenzy, screaming and yelling, Styx and his thugs quickly ran after the rats. As the Dredge left, the Spinners moved off in a diagonal direction and followed the Dredge at a safe distance.

Chapter 30
Trapped

Trapped

Meanwhile Princess Ariadne and her small band were moving at a fairly rapid pace, trying to vacate the Forgotten Land. Pello was bringing up the rear of the group, and he knew that they were being followed. A short time later, he heard a commotion like the trampling of feet.

Pello was very concerned because he knew that the cockroaches were pretty stealthy in their movements most of the time, and you would never hear them coming. He stopped, turned around, drew out his sword, and waited.

The wait was not long. Pello quickly turned and started running. While he was running, he yelled out, "Rats and cockroaches are charging at us. Run for your lives!"

The cockroaches were quickly overtaking Pello. As they were passing him, he was cutting as many of them down with his sword as he could, but their sheer numbers were too overwhelming.

Princess Ariadne looked at her small friends, who were sticking very close to her as she ran. Waving her arms as she ran, she said, "Go save yourselves. Get away while you can." She knew that Slink and Weezer could easily escape up the rock walls and that Tizzy could fly away.

Slink looked up at the princess and said, "Slink says, we will not leave your side, my princess."

Just then a cockroach jumped on the back of the princess. Slink leaped up and clamped down on the cockroach with his mouth and threw him aside, smashing him into the rocks.

The princess stopped and picked up Weezer. She gave him a hug and said, "Lead the Spinners away from here and show them the way back to Atlantis. Do not let the crystal fall into the hands of the Dredge." Weezer started to open his mouth, but the princess put her finger on his lips and said, "Not a word. Just go." She sat Weezer down on the cavern floor and ran off.

Weezer knew that it was no time to argue with the princess. He quickly hopped over to the Spinners and yelled, "The princess wants you to follow me. There is no time to waste." Without saying another word, he hopped off in another direction from where the princess was running.

Graham and Keno never got a chance to ask Weezer any questions. They simply veered off in the direction Weezer was hopping. To their amazement, none of the rats or cockroaches chose to follow them.

As the two kept running, they now realized that the princess was trying to separate herself from the crystal. If the crystal and the princess both fell into the hands of the Dredge, Atlantis was doomed. The two never looked back again; they just kept running and running.

Although Graham, Keno, and Weezer had made their escape, Pello, the princess, and Slink were now surrounded by the cockroaches and rats, and Tizzy was still flying overhead.

With his sword drawn, Pello looked over at Princess Ariadne and said, "When I engage these beasts, you and Slink make a run for it."

The princess nodded her head in approval. Pello raised his sword and started swinging like a madman. The princess and Slink began running as fast as they could. Pello had the cockroaches and rats backing up, and then out of nowhere, a poison spear ripped through his shoulder. He spun around and then keeled over on his side.

Seconds later Styx walked up to Pello's lifeless body and kicked it. He signaled his men to go catch the princess. Although the Dredge goons quickly caught the princess, Slink scurried off undetected into the rocks.

Two of Styx's goons threw the princess down in front of Styx. Styx looked at his goons and said, "That's no way to treat a princess."

He bent over and grabbed her by her collar and jerked her up to a standing position. He then added, "Now that's better."

He reached over and lifted up the princess's chin and added, "My little princess, you sure gave us a run. Now that the chase is over, we'll all go to Atlantis and watch its destruction."

Before he could say another word, a massive upheaval struck. A moment later it was over.

Now very angry, the princess yelled, "You fool, you're destroying all of the kingdoms, not just Atlantis. You're even going to destroy the surface world."

Styx laughed and said, "The kingdom of Atlantis will perish, but that's all." He went on to say, "That's enough talk. Let's move on to Atlantis."

The princess looked over at Pello and said, "Please remove the spear from my friend and save him."

Styx snapped back, "There's nothing I can do for him. That spear was poison, but you already know that, my dear." He jerked her by the arm and said, "Let's go!"

Styx finally had the prize he wanted. Now he and the Dredge goons were off to see the destruction of Atlantis. Blackie and his gang of rats and the packs of cockroaches had no desire to go to Atlantis. They'd had enough. It was time for them to go back to Undercroft.

At this point Styx couldn't care less. He had the princess, and soon he would see the destruction of Atlantis. The rats and the cockroaches turned and headed back to Undercroft, while the Dredge marched on.

Hours later Portagee, Sam, and Michael came upon the site where the princess had been captured. They found Pello lying on the ground. Tears began to flow down Sam's face. Michael gave her a hug and said, "He was a brave man and did not go down without a fight. We're all going to miss him."

Portagee walked over and bent down to get a closer look at Pello. He smiled and said, "I don't think we've lost our friend."

Sam lifted her head off Michael's shoulder and asked, "Why would you say that?"

Portagee replied, "Look at that spear. It must have been thrown so hard that it went all the way through his shoulder. Looks to me like it went so quickly through his shoulder that I think very little poison found its way into Pello."

He reached out and snapped the spear in half, and then Portagee pulled it out of Pello's shoulder. At that same moment, Pello's body flinched. Portagee added, "See. He's still very much alive."

Michael ripped off the sleeve of his shirt, handed it to Portagee, and said, "Here, use this to bandage his shoulder."

Sam stepped in. "Here, let me do it." She carefully bandaged his arm.

While she was doing that, Pello began to wake up. He opened his eyes and sat up. After looking around, he asked, "What happened? Where is the princess?"

Michael replied, "Portagee pulled a spear out of your shoulder. You're very lucky to be alive. We believe that the princess was taken prisoner." He then pointed. "They appear to be going in that direction."

Pello replied, "We must get going; they're taking her to Atlantis. I have failed her. I allowed her to be captured."

Michael said, "You didn't fail her. You went down fighting for her. Why would they be taking her to Atlantis? Isn't that what we wanted?"

As Pello stood up, he said, "The Dredge must think that they're going to finally destroy Atlantis by keeping the princess from repairing the pendulum." Pello bent down and picked up his sword and said, "We don't have a moment to lose." At a fast pace, he went off in the direction of Atlantis.

The three Spinners looked at each other and took off after Pello.

Chapter 31
The Last Stand

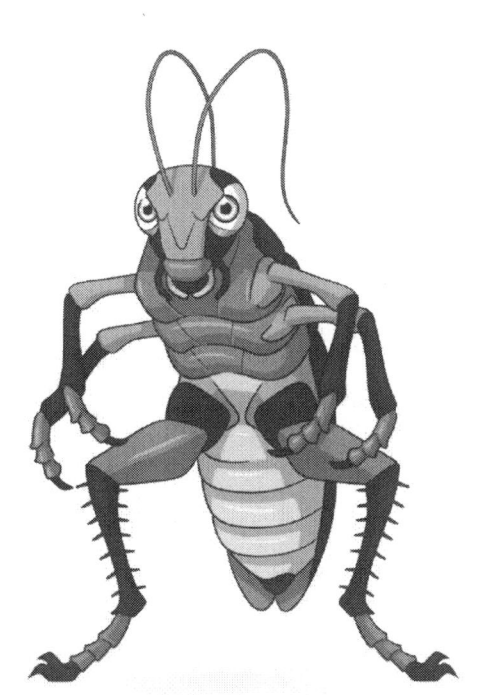

The Last Stand

The Dredge army, delivered by Claws and his fellow crabs, had laid an effective blockade of the city of Atlantis. The gates to the city were totally blocked. The inhabitants of Atlantis were in full-protection mode and were not about to allow the Dredge to overrun their city.

What they didn't know was that Styx had no intention of invading Atlantis. He was simply going to prevent the Atlanteans from leaving the city and let the upheavals destroy them.

A short time later, Styx and his regiment of goons joined his forces at the gates of Atlantis. Styx was very careful to keep the princess hidden away so that the inhabitants of Atlantis could not see her. He was fearful that if they did, they might try to rescue her.

To make matters worse for Atlantis, Claws and his band of ghost crabs also joined the Dredge at the walls. With the addition of the crabs, the Atlanteans' fate was sealed. There was no way that they would venture out of Atlantis to face the crabs.

Several hours later Keno, Graham, and Weezer made their way into the home cavern of Atlantis. They were moving very cautiously along the shoreline, especially now that they could see the Dredge and the giant crabs.

Weezer hopped up into Keno's arms and asked, "With all the Dredge mingling around, how can we ever find the princess?"

Before Keno could answer, Graham said, "Look up in the air. Tizzy is circling that area over there. That means that the princess is close by. She would never leave the princess's side."

Keno added, "That's good. Now we need to find a way into Atlantis and wait for Princess Ariadne to meet us in the Great Crystal Hall."

Weezer asked, "Why can't we get the princess on the way to the Great Crystal Hall?"

Graham replied, "The only time the crystal and the princess will be together is in the Great Crystal Hall. We can't let the Dredge capture the princess and the crystal." Graham looked down at Weezer and asked, "So can you get us to the Great Crystal Hall undetected?"

Weezer replied, "I can, but I'm not sure you can."

Keno asked, "What's that supposed to mean?"

Weezer wheezed a couple of times and said, "We're not going how the crow flies; we're going how the frog swims. Can you both swim and hold your breath?"

Keno and Graham both looked at each other and nodded their heads. Keno replied, "We're good, as long as I can fit my big body through the underwater passage."

Weezer, hopping up and down, said, "Well, let's go." He hopped off in the direction of Atlantis, with Graham and Keno following.

Moments later another upheaval struck with such severity that one of the walls of Atlantis collapsed into rubble. The Atlanteans quickly filled the voids in the wall; they waited for a Dredge attack, but it was not to be. The Dredge were going to wait and let the upheavals do their dirty work. Once Atlantis fell into ruin, they would overrun the magnificent city.

While Keno and Graham pondered what to do, Pello, Sam, Michael, and Portagee arrived at Atlantis from the other size of the massive cavern. To their surprise, Slink was there waiting for them. Slink looked at Pello and said, "Slink says, you four sure took your time getting here."

Out of breath and still in pain from his wound, Pello replied, "Forgive me, oh wondrous skink, but we were detained."

Slink went on to say, "Slink says, I know where the princess is, but getting to her will be tricky." His tail high in the air, Slink bent it and pointed it in her direction. He added, "Slink says, she's in the stone garden."

Pello looked at the others and said, "All we can do now is wait. Sooner or later the Dredge will have to sleep, and that's when we'll rescue the princess. We'll have to get her back into Atlantis and hopefully repair the pendulum before it's too late."

Sam added, "That works, as long as Keno and Graham are there, waiting for us."

Michael replied, "They'll be there." They all sat down behind a rock formation and waited for the right moment.

Meanwhile Styx had met with his goons and sent many of them out in all directions to make sure that there would be no surprises. Styx continued to meet with some of his lieutenants.

He said, "The end of Atlantis is near. I can taste it. You can see that their walls are crumbling. We have the will and the means to destroy Atlantis. Without a crystal and their beloved princess, they are a doomed kingdom. We will wait, and when the time is right, we will invade and crush them."

Styx pounded his fist on a nearby rock, and as he stormed away, he turned and pointed at the princess and said, "Don't let her out of your sight!" He stormed off in the direction of Claws and his crabs.

To the surprise of Keno and Graham, Weezer was moving along the shoreline and not heading toward Atlantis. Graham asked as he pointed, "Weezer, aren't we supposed to be going in that direction?"

Weezer smiled and said, "Just follow me, my friends. You'll soon find out."

Chapter 32
The Final Upheaval

The Final Upheaval

A short time later, Weezer came to a spot where the rocky shoreline was very damp. You could actually see water trickling out of the rocks. He pointed down at the rocks and said, "This is the way in to Atlantis."

Keno laughed and said, "My little friend, you've got to be kidding."

Weezer was not laughing. He replied, "This is freshwater from above, not saltwater. This is water that flows through the palace garden. Since my toes aren't made for digging into rocks, would you both start digging this rock out?" Weezer added, "Be careful; I don't want you two to get too wet."

Graham smiled as he started digging in the loose rocks. He replied, "This little stream of water is not going to get us wet." Graham and Keno continued to dig on for another twenty minutes as Weezer looked for signs of the Dredge or packs of cockroaches.

Finally they were down to one fairly large rock that appeared to block the flow of the stream from the palace garden. Graham looked at Keno and asked, "Hey, big guy, can you give me a hand pulling this rock out?"

Keno replied, "Sure."

They both begin tugging at the rock, but it was not budging. Weezer whispered, "Be careful boys."

Just as Keno was about to reply, another huge upheaval struck. The ground shook, and as the two Spinners were falling back, the rock dislodged and flew out directly at them. A second later a massive wall of water exploded out of the hole and sent Keno and Graham flying head over heels into the lake behind them.

Weezer went into the water right after them. Keno was lying face down in the water, while Graham was trying to stand up, coughing and choking. Weezer immediately tried to roll Keno over on his back, but he was too small to get the job done.

Finally Graham quit coughing up water and got his bearings back. He saw that Keno was in trouble. He reached out and rolled Keno onto his back and pulled him ashore. Fortunately Keno was only knocked out and had not swallowed any water. Keno came to immediately.

After a few minutes of resting, Keno looked over to where they had been removing rocks and said, "Look, Graham. There's a tunnel over there. We must have drained a pond in the palace garden."

Weezer jumped up and down said, "I told you so! I told you so!"

The three walked over to the tunnel. It was big enough for both of the Spinners to crawl through on their hands and knees. Graham looked at Weezer and said, "Good, mate, you're the smallest. You lead the way, and we'll follow."

Weezer replied, "OK, follow me." He hopped into the tunnel and was out of sight in minutes.

Keno said, "You'd better go next, just in case the tunnel gets too small for me."

Graham replied, "Let's go." Graham got down on his hands and knees and went into the tunnel. Keno followed in right behind him.

Meanwhile the other three Spinners and Pello had fallen asleep. Pello felt something sticky and wet on his face and abruptly awoke from his nap. As he opened his eyes, he saw two big eyes staring back at him. He quickly sat up and said, "What is it, Slink?"

Slink replied, "Slink says, the guards and the princess are asleep."

Pello replied, "That's good news; we must act quickly and rescue Princess Ariadne. Go ahead and wake the others." Slink's sticky tongue got to work fast. Seconds later the Spinners were up on their feet and ready to go.

Pello looked at the others and said, "We only have one chance to free the princess and save Atlantis. Follow me, single file, and be ready for anything."

Pello signaled Slink with his hand to show him the way. Slink slithered out over the rocky terrain, with Pello and the Spinners following.

Slink was right; except for the Dredge watching the Atlantis walls, or lack of them, the rest of the Dredge army was asleep. It had been a big night of gorging on mold, roots, and bugs.

As they crept by the sleeping Dredge goons, Sam whispered to the others, "How gross. I would die if I had to eat any of that."

At that moment, a voice said, "Maybe you should."

A Dredge goon had just woken up and had heard Sam. Before he could say another word, Michael gave the goon a roundhouse punch in the face and sent the goon stumbling backward. Portagee had managed to drop on all fours behind him, and as the goon fell backward, he tripped over Portagee and was out like a baby by the time he hit the ground.

A surprised Sam gave Michael and Portagee each a big hug. The group continued on and tried not to wake any more Dredge. The next big fear Pello had was that one big upheaval would wake the entire camp of the Dredge.

As they made their way into the area where Princess Ariadne was being held, Slink saw her first and was about to run and greet her with plenty of sticky licks when Pello grabbed him by the tail and said, "Not so fast, my friend. You'll scare her to death. You stay here, and I'll wake her up very gently."

Slink stopped in his tracks while Pello made his way to the princess. He placed his hand over her mouth, which caused her to flinch. As soon as she saw Pello, the princess relaxed, and Pello removed his hand from her mouth. Pello waved to the others to follow him and the princess as they made a beeline toward Atlantis.

Everything was going according to plan. They were not far away from the gates of Atlantis when the unthinkable happened. Another massive upheaval struck, knocking everyone to the ground. Not only was the upheaval devastating but also Pello's worse fear came true. The entire camp of the Dredge was awakened. Pello jumped to his feet and yelled out, "Run for the gates!"

A few of the Dredge had figured out what had happened and were in hot pursuit; however, that was not the obstacle confronting them. To their dismay, they saw the giant crab, Claws, standing between them and the gates of Atlantis. Not to mention that the Dredge were closing in on them from behind.

Sam looked around and said, "Oh, lord, are we ever going to get a break?"

Portagee yelled out, "Try to run under him!"

The two Spinners ran at Claws, while Pello pulled out his sword and started swinging it at Claws's legs. Claws swatted Pello out of the way with one of his claws, and with his other huge claw, he picked up Michael and Portagee and swung them around like paper dolls.

Princess Ariadne stepped forward and said, "Take me. I'm the one you want. Let my friends go." Claws paid little to no attention to the princess; something else had grabbed his attention.

There was a disturbing squawking and flapping sound coming from overhead. Claws's instincts were now taking over. He had no natural enemies in this world, but in the surface world, his most feared enemy was the sea gull. Claws was struck with fear. He quickly dropped the Spinners, and with the rest of his crabs, he ran for the only protection they could find, the lake.

Princess Ariadne looked up into the air and smiled. It was Tizzy. Tizzy flew down and landed on the shoulder of the princess. The surprised princess asked, "What were those sounds you were making?"

Tizzy replied, "I was imitating a sea gull. On the surface world, they like to eat crabs."

The princess gave Tizzy a hug and added, "Well done."

Sam rushed up. "The Dredge evidently aren't scared by sea gulls and are coming fast. I think we should go now."

With no more delays, the small group ran through the severely damaged gates to Atlantis. Seconds later another severe upheaval struck and caused more damage to Atlantis.

As soon as the upheaval ended, a group of sentries rushed to Pello and the princess. One sentry asked, "What is your command, Pello? Do you want us to stop the Dredge at the gates?"

Pello turned to the princess. She replied instead of Pello. "Take my people to the outskirts of Atlantis and wait. This battle will be won or lost in the Great Crystal Hall. In the meantime, keep my people safe. You'll know if and when it will be safe to come back. Now go!"

The sentries ran off to evacuate the population of Atlantis as quickly as possible. The small group ran toward the Great Crystal Hall, the Dredge army not far behind.

Chapter 33
The Crystal Spinner

The Crystal Spinner

Weezer, Graham, and Keno were still crawling through the tunnel and heading to the palace garden. The farther they went, the narrower the tunnel became. Weezer and Graham were doing fine; however, Keno could feel the tunnel closing in on him, and he was getting slightly claustrophobic.

Finally Keno said, "You guys, take the crystal and go on without me. I don't think I can make it much farther."

Weezer yelled back to Keno, "Don't stop now; we're almost there." Keno nodded his head in agreement, but he really didn't know if he could make it.

Minutes later the tunnel turned upward; Weezer had been right. They came out in the bottom of an empty pond in the middle of the palace garden. As Graham helped pull Keno out of the tunnel, he gasped for air. Once out of the tunnel, Keno lay on his back for a few minutes.

Weezer interrupted Keno's state of rest. "We need to go now if we're going to beat the Dredge to the Great Crystal Hall." Keno stood up and followed Graham and Weezer.

Meanwhile Princess Ariadne and the others had already made it to the Great Crystal Hall. It was quickly evident that the other two Spinners and Weezer had not made it to the hall yet.

As they stood around, Michael said, "I hope nothing bad has happened to them."

Portagee added, "Princess, I'm a fixer. Maybe I can fix the pendulum."

The princess walked over to Michael and Portagee and replied, "That's a nice gesture, but only I can do this."

A voice from across the Great Hall added, "That's right, people, and that's not going to happen. We've got the hall surrounded, and there will be no new crystal pendulum."

It was Styx. The entire hall was now surrounded by his Dredge goons. The end appeared to be near for Atlantis.

The princess replied, "If I don't restore the crystal pendulum, the Dredge will also be destroyed."

Styx yelled back, "You lie! You're all a bunch of cowards. Your world is about to come to an end."

Another upheaval erupted, almost causing the Great Crystal Hall to collapse.

While all the commotion was going on in the hall, Weezer, Graham, and Keno arrived. Looking around, Graham said, "It's apparent that we're a little late." He asked Weezer, "Is there a way to get into the hall?"

Weezer replied, "Yes, but I have a better idea. Just follow me." Weezer hopped around to where there was a crystal ladder leading to the top of the structure. He immediately started climbing the ladder.

Once Keno and Graham made their way to the ladder, Keno asked, "Do you think this crystal ladder is safe?"

Graham replied, "There's only one way to find out."

He started climbing up the ladder after Weezer. Keno waited for a couple of minutes and followed behind Graham. Once they were at the top, they entered a window that led them out onto a massive beam with a cable secured to it. On the other end would be the crystal.

Keno looked down and said, "I'm not sliding down that cable to secure the crystal to it."

Graham replied, "Weezer is a genius. We can't go down there, but the end of the cable can come up to us. Just do it slowly, and maybe the Dredge won't notice." After Graham called him a genius, Weezer was all smiles.

Below, everyone was recovering from the upheaval, and the standoff still existed. Graham was right; so far no one down below had noticed the cable being pulled up into the loft. That is, except for Princess Ariadne. She had already sensed Weezer, Keno, and Graham above her.

Meanwhile, trying to protect the princess, Pello faced off with Styx. Styx was so confident that he kept his supporting cast of goons well behind him. He was twice the size of Pello and was ready to crush him. Styx kept swinging his poison lionfish spear at Pello. More agile, Pello evaded contact with the poisonous spear.

Finally Pello got in a swing with his sword and sliced through the tip of the spear. The surprise swing from Pello did not slow Styx down. He flipped his spear up in the air and grabbed it by the end that had been cut off, and with a full swing, he smashed the blunt end of the spear on the side of Pello's face, sending him flying across the great hall.

While all this was going on, Graham and Keno had pulled the end of the cable up to them and secured the crystal to it. Just as they were lowering the crystal, another upheaval struck and caused Keno and Graham to fall from the platform. Graham managed to grab the cable and stop his fall, while Keno was in a free-fall state.

Since the princess was in the Great Crystal Hall, she was at full power. Not taking her eyes off Styx, she raised her right arm into the air and slowed Keno's fall into a slow-motion fall; he landed on the floor of the hall like it was a pillow.

Graham quickly slid down the cable, while Portagee and Sam ran over to Pello. Styx now understood why Princess

Ariadne had wanted her last stand to be in the Great Crystal Hall.

Styx yelled out, "You can play all the games you want, but I will still destroy you all."

As Styx stepped closer to the princess, Michael charged at him. Michael ran his shoulder into the belly of Styx and just simply bounced off him. Michael's head hit the floor, and he was out cold.

For the first time, Styx saw the uncut crystal dangling from the cable. He yelled out to his goon, "Destroy that crystal!"

The Dredge goons charged at the crystal, but before they could reach it, the princess raised both hands high into the air and sent the crystal spinning a hundred miles per hour around the room, hitting every goon who neared it.

The spinning of the crystal also caused massive upheavals. The Crystal Great Hall was beginning to show fractures in its walls.

In desperation, Styx picked up two poison spears and charged at the princess. The princess had no time to react or to protect herself. As she fell backward, Styx tripped over Slink, fell on top of the princess, and sent both of them to the floor. Then Graham, Sam, and Portagee ran to the princess's rescue, but the massive body of Styx completely covered her.

Everything went quiet for a few moments, and then a faint sound was heard. Sam yelled out, "Help me move this big goon! I think I heard the princess!"

The Spinners lifted Styx from one side and rolled him off the princess. The princess had managed to raise her hands high enough to create a small force field to turn the spears back toward Styx. In the fall, he had impaled himself on his own spears.

Seconds later Styx's body turned to a blackish-gray smoke, and he vaporized. The rest of the Dredge goons saw this and ran for their lives back toward Undercroft.

A short time later, Princess Ariadne was back on her feet and helped bring Pello and Michael back to consciousness. She turned back to the crystal and placed it directly over the razor-sharp, triangular, pointed, black, magnetic stone and gave it a spin. In seconds, the uncut crystal became a perfect inverted-triangle crystal pendulum. The points of the stone and crystal were touching and in perfect alignment.

Princess Ariadne turned to the Spinners and said, "I christen this crystal pendulum the Crystal Spinner, named after my good friends who came to the aid of Atlantis in our darkest hour."

The Spinners, Princess Ariadne, Pello, Slink, Weezer, and Tizzy all came together for a big family hug.

Chapter 34
Homeward Bound

Homeward Bound

Several days had passed. There was no sign of the Dredge, the crabs, or the lionfish. The Crystal Pendulum had brought peace and stability back to Atlantis. The Spinners finally had time to see the real beauty of the kingdom of Atlantis.

Later that day Princess Ariadne met with the Spinners in the restored palace garden. Pello, Slink, Weezer, and Tizzy also joined them.

After greeting the Spinners, the princess said, "We have loved having you here, but I know that you are homesick and your families are missing you. I wish you could stay and see my coronation in a few days, but I know that's impossible."

Sam stepped forward and replied, "Yes, we do need to go home now, but maybe someday we can return."

With a slight smile and a few tears, the princess added, "I would like that very much, but as time passes, you all will have to move on and forget about us."

She paused for a moment and added, "Enough of this sadness. I have arranged for your transportation home, and Pello will escort you."

She looked over at Tizzy and added, "Tizzy, you came here with the Spinners, and I'm sure you also want to go back home."

Tizzy flew over and landed in the princess's lap and said, "This is my home now. I will stay here."

Princess Ariadne stood up and said, "Well, so be it. Now, follow me, and I'll show you your transportation home."

To the surprise of the Spinners, as they walked through the gates of Atlantis, they saw Snorkel the sea turtle waiting for them at the shoreline of the lake. The princess could not bear to say good-bye again and stayed at the gates of Atlantis with her three little friends and waved good-bye. She knew in her heart that they would never return.

As the Spinners neared Snorkel, he said, "Welcome! All aboard for your scenic trip back to beautiful Bermuda." He laid his head down on the shore and added, "Watch your step, please."

The Spinners knew the drill and climbed up on his head and made their way up under his shell. Pello joined them, and they all waved good-bye to the princess.

Just as Snorkel was about to push off, Slink, Weezer, and Tizzy crawled under his shell. Slink said, "Slink says, I will miss you all." Before the Spinners could reply, he gave them all a sloppy, sticky lick.

Tizzy flickered around them and gave them all butterfly kisses with her wings, and Weezer wheezed out a little song for them. As quickly as they arrived, the three little friends left.

Snorkel shoved off and submerged under the water; he was very careful that they would have a large air pocket to breath. Ten minutes later Snorkel surfaced on an isolated beach on the south shore of Bermuda.

As they ran ashore, a puzzled Portagee turned back to Pello, who was still standing on snorkel's head, and asked, "I think we have a problem here. How can we go home if we're only two inches tall?"

Pello's face turned red. In a very embarrassed tone, he said, "Oh, I almost forgot to turn you back into giants again." He pulled out a small crystal from his pocket and said, "Are you ready?"

Sam replied, "Yes, but how can we get back in touch with you and the princess when we want to return to Atlantis?"

With a sad look on his face, Pello said, "When I return you to your normal size, this adventure will be a distant dream to you. You may retain a few threads of Atlantis in your thoughts, but that is all."

Before the Spinners could say anything, he pointed the crystal at them and cast a wavy, pulsating light. They all blacked out.

One after another, the Spinners began to wake up. Michael was the first to sit up in the sand and said, "Look at what time it is. We'd better be getting home."

Sam added, "Yeah, but I don't even remember coming to the beach. We don't even have our swimsuits on."

Their conversation just became more confusing. Finally Keno said, "We'd better get up to the bus stop on South Shore and get home before it gets dark." One after another, the Spinners trekked up through the sand dunes to the bus stop.

None of them noticed that they were all being watched from the ocean by Pello and Snorkel. Pello tapped Snorkel on the head and said, "They're safe now. It's time for us to go home to Atlantis."

Snorkel sank under the waves and was gone in an instant. Only time would tell if the Spinners would have another adventure in Atlantis.

About the Author

R. C. Farrington

Author R. C. Farrington, a Benton, Louisiana, resident, travels extensively to Bermuda, the setting for most of his novels, which combine action and adventure with historical and geographical accuracy.

Farrington, an award-winning author known for his Spinners trilogy, enjoys exploring old forts, deserted islands, jungles, and caves. He fills his novels with blockade runners, sharks, pirates, and terrorists. Several of his novels have won the Shreveport-Bossier Regional ADDY awards.

More novels by R. C. Farrington

Bayou Banditos
Shadows of Black Bayou

The Bayou Banditos are at it again. From the swamps of Louisiana, they've tracked and captured murderers, bank robbers, and drug smugglers in places where no law-enforcement officials would dare go for years.

Working for the FBI, the Bayou Banditos are tracking a gun-smuggling biker gang when all hell breaks loose. They find themselves facing an army of Russian mercenaries hired to assassinate them. With members of their family kidnapped and held deep within the swamps of Louisiana, the banditos must deliver the ransom, which is not money but themselves.

The Bayou Banditos—Buck, Bubba, JRod, and Portagee—are a father-and-sons team of trackers. They each have their own unique skill set, which makes them an unpredictable force to contend with. Their weapons and firearms are for the most part relics of the past, but suited for their style and the conditions in which they work.

There is no room for mistakes in this life-and-death struggle for survival.

The Life and Times of the Bayou Banditos

From the swamps of Louisiana, the Bayou Banditos for years have tracked and captured murderers, bank robbers, and drug smugglers in places where no law-enforcement officials would dare go. From the swamps of the South to mountainous terrains of the Rockies, these unorthodox trackers will go anywhere to track down their targets. The news organizations call them lawless bounty hunters. Law-enforcement agencies despise them, but they are needed for their unusual tracking talents.

The Bayou Banditos, Buck, Bubba, JRod, and Portagee, are a father and sons team of trackers. They each have their own unique skill set, which makes them an unpredictable force to contend with. Their weapons and firearms are for the most part relics of the past but suited for their style and the conditions in which they work.

The Bayou Banditos now find themselves in the undesirable position of being hunted. Trapped in the jungles of a foreign country, they are considered assassins, with drug-cartel death squads tracking them. If the death squads don't kill them, the beasts of the jungle will. There is no room for mistakes in this life-and-death struggle for survival.

Blood Fangs
Samantha Savage Beast Huntress—Episode II

A demonic clan of blood beasts has lured huntress Samantha Savage out of her safe haven in the Bermuda Triangle. Having been ravenously attacked and bitten by a blood beast herself, she is now determined to eradicate these beasts from the earth. Driven by this quest, she will have to rely on her newfound powers and self-control to fend off the demons that flow deep within her body. Her mission in life is to track down and destroy the blood clans of the world.

The powerful blood beast Delphine, masquerading as the Voodoo Queen of New Orleans, has wreaked havoc on the post-Katrina inhabitants of the city in recent years. The beast huntress has left the island of Bermuda with her inventive partner, Portagee, to enter the world of dark bayous, gators, and blood beasts in order to search out and destroy the Queen of Voodoo and her clan.

The blood beasts call Samantha the Day Walker and will stop at nothing to turn her into one of their own or destroy her. Outnumbered fifty to one, the beast huntress will have to stalk her prey in the deadly swamps of Louisiana and the dark shadows of the New Orleans French Quarter. This will truly be the battle of the beauty and the beasts.

Blood Fangs
Quest for the Dark One—Episode I

It is the year of our lord 1629. For over one hundred years, Zuka, dark prince of the jungle, and his blood beasts have ravaged the local native tribes deep within the Congo jungle.

Ambushed by one of the neighboring tribes, Zuka and his vampire clan are trapped and caged like animals and then rafted down the Congo River to an awaiting slave ship that will take them to the New World. After they enter the unknown turbulent waters of the Bermuda Triangle, a horrific hurricane breaks *Bad Blood*, their ship, to pieces and transports the few survivors into the parallel world of the Bermuda Triangle.

For hundreds of years, these vampires have plundered and killed the lost inhabitants in the Bermuda Triangle. Zuka and his clan of blood beasts are determined to find a portal back to the present-day world in order to avenge his betrayal and wreak havoc on an unsuspecting population as they search for a dark queen.

This rare strain of blood beasts has very extraordinary powers that make them almost indestructible. There is no end to their thirst for blood.

After a ten-year absence from the Bermuda Triangle, the Spinners (from the Spinners Trilogy) are now young adults and must return to the Triangle to help their friends. They have to stop the blood beasts before they can find the gateway that allows them to return to the world they were banished from almost four hundred years ago.

The Spinners will only have one chance to stop these beasts. In this epic battle of human versus blood beast, there can just be one survivor.

Awards
Quest for the Dark One was awarded the Shreveport-Bossier regional 2012 Bronze ADDY award.

Phantom Marauders of the Bermuda Triangle

Drug lords who will stop at nothing to distribute their illegal drugs have law-enforcement officials around the world outgunned, outnumbered, and sometimes outwitted. They have made a mockery out of the criminal-justice system and are winning the war on drugs.

In response to this failure of law enforcement and the criminal-justice system, a desperate plan to eradicate drug trafficking has been conceived of on the tiny island of Bermuda. With the aid of the United States, the island's governor has declared war on the drug lords of South America and the Caribbean.

By issuing a long-forgotten license to privateers to seek and destroy drug smugglers with no legal entanglements, the governor has leveled the playing field of the war on drugs. This Letter of Marque to privateers encompasses the waters of the Bermuda Triangle. These marauders now have the license to attack and destroy drug trafficking enemies of the state.

Although the Treaty of Paris of 1856 has long since banned privateering, the United States never signed the treaty. In fact, the US Constitution still to this day permits Letters of Marque and Reprisal.

Turk Black, the captain of the ghost ship *The Phantom*, and his crew of Bermudians and Americans are hell-bent on wreaking havoc on drug trafficking in the Atlantic Ocean.

Not since Blackbeard, with his ship *Queen Anne's Revenge*, has there been so much terror and destruction on the open seas.

With bounties on their heads and no safe ports to enter, *The Phantom* and her crew are marked by death squads of the drug cartels. Outnumbered one hundred to one, *The Phantom* and her crew play a deadly cat-and-mouse game using modern technology to evade, track, and destroy the drug traffickers. The tide is about to turn.

Awards
Phantom Marauders of the Bermuda Triangle was awarded the Shreveport-Bossier regional 2012 Bronze ADDY award.

Death Diamonds of Bermúdez

Hell-bent on establishing an independent Boer Nation, modern-day Apartheid mercenaries from South Africa will stop at nothing to ignite their coup d'etat. Finding the Death Diamonds is the final piece of their diabolical puzzle.

A small group of renegade Boer War soldiers imprisoned in Bermuda in the early twentieth century discovered the treasures of Bermúdez but never revealed the location. With the most evil intentions, their descendants have searched for the Death Diamonds of the lost city of Bermúdez to this day.

FBI Special Agent Derrick Storm and Bermuda's Inspector Ian Savage are the only ones who have any chance of keeping these ruthless mercenaries from fulfilling their diabolical scheme. Outgunned and outmanned, Savage and Storm must rely on their gut instincts to outwit these killers.

The Spinners (from the Spinners Trilogy) find themselves drawn into a treasure hunt cloaked with deceit and deception. Somehow Savage, Storm, and the Spinners must find the Death Diamonds first and prevent a nightmare of death and destruction.

Awards
Death Diamonds of Bermudez was awarded the Shreveport-Bossier regional 2009 Silver ADDY award.

The Isle of Devils Holy War

The most explosive terrorist plot in history is about to become a reality.

A secret terrorist organization has used the Western world's greed for oil to cloak its holy war. Undercover agents try to expose the terrorists' plot on the island of Bermuda before thousands of innocent lives are lost.

FBI Agent Derrick Storm from the United States, with the assistance of Ian Savage, a police inspector from Bermuda, attempts to uncover the most sophisticated and deadly terrorist plot ever set in motion. FBI Agent Storm is one of the top law-enforcement specialists in the United States. He has a great respect for the law but will bend the rules if necessary to apprehend criminals.

Inspector Savage has a school-of-hard-knocks law-enforcement degree. By Bermuda's police standards, his actions are often unorthodox. In spite of that, he's one of the most effective crime fighters in Bermuda.

Somehow these two agents from different races, backgrounds, and countries must work together to derail a terrorist plot that grows into a serious threat to the security of the world.

Awards
The Isle of Devil's Holy War was awarded the Shreveport-Bossier regional 2008 Gold ADDY award.

Spinners
The Lost Treasure of Bermuda—Episode I

In this first episode, five teenagers unlock the secrets of the Bermuda Triangle, where the past and the present collide. The Lost Treasure of Bermuda has intrigued and eluded treasure hunters for more than two hundred years. The Spinners have to face and survive evil villains in Bermuda and in the Bermuda Triangle who will stop at nothing to control the Tucker Cross and the Lost Treasure.

Spinners
The Protectors of the Bermuda Triangle— Episode II

Five teenagers from Bermuda are trapped in the Bermuda Triangle. They must face the forces of evil to protect the Triangle from destruction. Scarzo, a modern-day mercenary from Brazil, kidnaps the Spinners and is determined to force them to reveal the secret gateway to the Bermuda Triangle. The Spinners also have the bad fortune of crossing paths with Scorpion, a Voodoo pirate from Haiti. She will stop at nothing to find the power source that controls the Bermuda Triangle.

Spinners
The Curse of the Bermuda Abyss—Episode III

Five teenagers trapped in the Bermuda Triangle find themselves drawn into the dark depths of the Bermuda Abyss. In this third episode, the Spinners may have finally met their match as they face the most vicious and most notorious evil being of all time. In a race for their lives and with very little time, the Spinners must escape from the depths of the Bermuda Abyss and its curse.

Made in the USA
Middletown, DE
21 November 2016